Bolan's p[...] up the man in the doorway

The Executioner knew the type—dangerous, but not a real pro. It was one thing to gun down an innocent civilian. It was something entirely different to go against a trained fighter.

An engine revved, and the backup car slowly turned the corner, approaching the hitter from behind. He stepped forward, firing a trio of shots at his target—but Bolan was already in motion.

The warrior had dived sideways a split second before the assassin made his move, reading the tension in the man's jerky movements. Bolan ripped the Beretta free and triggered a three-round burst that stitched a perfect triangle over the gunner's heart.

At the same time, another shot from across the street cored the man's temple, kicking him sideways.

The Executioner's shoulder hit the ground at the end of the dive, then he was up and scrambling into one of the narrow alleys that splintered the block.

The backup car squealed to a stop.

MACK BOLAN®

The Executioner

DON PENDLETON'S
THE EXECUTIONER®
FEATURING MACK BOLAN®

PHANTOM FORCE

A GOLD EAGLE BOOK FROM
WORLDWIDE®

TORONTO • NEW YORK • LONDON • PARIS
AMSTERDAM • STOCKHOLM • HAMBURG
ATHENS • MILAN • TOKYO • SYDNEY

First edition December 1991

ISBN 0-373-61156-0

Special thanks and acknowledgment to
Rich Rainey for his contribution to this work.

PHANTOM FORCE

Printed in U.S.A.

Leave not a stain in thine honor.

—Ecclesiasticus 33:22

Remember the past: let the elder men among us
emulate their own earlier deeds, and the younger
who are sons of those valiant fathers do their best
not to tarnish the virtues of their race.

—Pagondas of Thebes, 424 B.C.

Honor and tradition should be part of what makes
us who we are. But when a petty tyrant's perverted
sense of values provoke a confrontation, I'll meet the
challenge—head-on.

—Mack Bolan

THE
MACK BOLAN®
LEGEND

Nothing less than a war could have fashioned the destiny of the man called Mack Bolan. Bolan earned the Executioner title in the jungle hell of Vietnam.

But this soldier also wore another name—Sergeant Mercy. He was so tagged because of the compassion he showed to wounded comrades-in-arms and Vietnamese civilians.

Mack Bolan's second tour of duty ended prematurely when he was given emergency leave to return home and bury his family, victims of the Mob. Then he declared a one-man war against the Mafia.

He confronted the Families head-on from coast to coast, and soon a hope of victory began to appear. But Bolan had broken society's every rule. That same society started gunning for this elusive warrior—to no avail.

So Bolan was offered amnesty to work within the system against terrorism. This time, as an employee of Uncle Sam, Bolan became Colonel John Phoenix. With a command center at Stony Man Farm in Virginia, he and his new allies—Able Team and Phoenix Force—waged relentless war on a new adversary: the KGB.

But when his one true love, April Rose, died at the hands of the Soviet terror machine, Bolan severed all ties with Establishment authority.

Now, after a lengthy lone-wolf struggle and much soul-searching, the Executioner has agreed to enter an "arm's-length" alliance with his government once more, reserving the right to pursue personal missions in his Everlasting War.

1

The abandoned Shinto shrine stood regally above the snowcapped countryside, the remnants of its splinter-thin walls affording a solid view of anyone approaching—except for the phantomlike white shape that crept slowly uphill.

The intruder was camouflaged in arctic warfare gear, a reversible white suit that blended in with the icy terrain he prowled. Though spring had come to most of Japan, winter lingered on Hokkaido, the northernmost of the main islands, especially in the higher altitudes.

Mack Bolan had become part of the white landscape. A hooded smock covered his face, and a white elastic stretch cloth covered his pack. Even the sniper rifle he carried had been painted white.

He continued his uphill climb against the blustering wind that swept down the craggy face of the mountain, howling like a chorus of wolves.

The warrior paused for a brief rest when he neared a jagged clump of gray rocks. The air was thinner this high up, and his breath was shorter. His skin was wet and raw, and his lips were iced. He'd forced himself to move slowly and steadily to conserve his energy, but now the elements were taking their toll. Unless he went into action soon, the weather would be the ultimate winner.

He stretched his arms and legs, uncoiling the muscles that had grown tense and strained from the arduous trek uphill. It didn't help matters that he constantly had to look over his shoulder in case one of the perimeter guards had detected his presence.

It would have been safer to take out the guards first, but there were too many of them to do it quietly. The skirmish would have alerted the man he was gunning for, Ieyasu Kuro, the man who unknowingly waited in the mountain shrine for an uninvited guest.

Kuro was expecting a payoff from a Japanese-American defense conglomerate that his people had infiltrated. Working jointly on the development of kinetic weaponry and a space plane that could handle a number of space shuttle missions at a fraction of the present cost, the high-tech project drew some of the best minds from both countries to its research center north of Tokyo.

It attracted military consultants, scientists, spooks of all stripes and highly skilled engineers—people out to reshape the world.

It also attracted men like Kuro, who were all too willing to tear it down.

Kuro's clan had already killed one American technician and threatened to kill another unless their ransom demands were met. In return for an extortionate fortune, they promised to return the classified technical manual they'd stolen and drop the matter completely. No more killings, no more thefts.

Some negotiators might have accepted such a deal, but the negotiator Uncle Sam brought in was the Executioner.

That was one advantage Bolan had going for him as he closed in on the mountain stronghold. Kuro was expecting tribute, not retribution.

Bolan moved on again, giving the rocks a wide berth. His white silhouette against the gray rock would be a dead giveaway, with the accent on dead.

The man at the shrine was no apprentice, nor was he a priest or monk. Kuro was a warrior. And though he fought for an underground army, one of the crime clans that plagued Japan, his skills were no less legitimate.

The incline rose sharply now, forcing Bolan to look up at a severe angle as he neared his target.

Sunlight glinted at the top of the shrine, blinding him momentarily. Then a barricade of clouds passed high overhead and spared his eyesight.

A curtain of windblown snow swirled around the shrine, and streams of smoke billowed from the chimney of a cottage immediately behind it. Unlike the other collapsing cottages that flanked the shrine, with roofless bedrooms and broken hearths, this one was more or less intact.

The smoke scattered the moment it escaped the chimney, chomped by the biting wind. The scent of wood smoke was strong, though. Bolan could almost see and feel the crackling fire, so urgent was his body's desire to get out of the icy air.

Abandoned, he thought, studying the shrine and the outbuildings. In terms of maintenance the place looked as if it was rarely inhabited. But the shrine was frequently used by members of the clan as an isolated drop site and a temporary hideout for Kuro while his minions went about the business of murder and ransom.

It was lived in, just as he'd been told.

As Bolan watched puffs of smoke drift from the chimney like dying breaths, he knew that would change soon.

As he moved closer through the snow, he saw the outline of a man sitting by the hearth.

It was too good to be true. Though the warrior unslung his sniper rifle, he didn't really believe his quarry would be so foolish as to make himself such an easy target.

The whisper of steel sliding from a sheath told him that his instincts were right.

There was no monopoly on stealth on the mountain.

His subconscious had already prepared him for such a possibility, propelling his body to the right in a dive through the snow. He tumbled through the cloud-light drifts, submerging out of sight. At the same time his gloved hands gripped the rifle like a staff. There was no time to fire. No time to flee. Only time to fight.

Bolan whirled around, wheeling the rifle in front of him as he rose into a half crouch. His right knee was on the ground, his foot pressed straight out on the slippery snow. His left leg was bent, firmly planted.

Like an iron statue rising from the snow, he met his opponent head-on.

"Hai!" The shout was as cold as the frozen hills around him.

Except for a slight flash of sunlight on the polished steel, the Executioner couldn't see the blade. He could sense it, though, by the man's movement.

The sword bit into the rifle, jarring Bolan's hands. He pushed himself to his feet a split second later, still keeping contact with his opponent's weapon. Then he pushed down hard, smashing the rifle stock into the man's nose.

Gouts of blood exploded from the guy's face and cascaded down his white parka before spattering the snow in a violent red rain.

His nose shattered by the blow, he reeled backward, instinctively staying close so the rifle couldn't be fired at him. He'd retained his grip on his sword, and black steel shone from his eyes.

A blood-specked, mustached grin spread across the man's face, as though he were almost pleased at the resistance he'd met.

He'd expected an easy kill, a perfunctory slaying. Now he adjusted his position and prepared to attack with a final sword thrust.

Bolan was tempted to step back, cradle the Accuracy International sniper rifle and trigger a 7.62 mm thrust of his own. But an accomplished swordsman could close the gap in time to make the rifle a harmless crutch. The man wielding the katana, a deadly combat sword, had obviously used it for more than just ceremony. The Executioner stayed his ground.

Kuro feinted with a slash at his abdomen, then reversed the sword so that the cutting edge faced skyward and the point of the blade was heading for Bolan's face.

The Executioner spun the rifle barrel downward with his left hand and whipped the stock into the side of the sword with his right, pushing it down as if he were sledgehammering a spike into the ground. The smack of metal on metal rang loudly until Kuro's blade sliced through the snow to the ground.

Bolan snapped an inside roundhouse kick to the Japanese's face, connecting solidly between Kuro's shoulder blade and head. He continued the attack, knowing that unless he stayed on the offensive the swordsman would catch him with a killing strike.

The moment the warrior's right foot touched earth again, he wheeled around and launched a hook kick to Kuro's hips. It wasn't a blow that could kill, more like a positioning strike that pushed the man off balance and prevented him from unleashing a fatal slash.

Now the Japanese clansman understood that the fight wasn't one-sided, that indeed he could fall off the mountain into the land of the gods and his ancestors.

"Amerikan-jin bushi," Kuro said, nodding his awareness of Bolan's martial skills. He appeared to move in slow motion as he held the sword in front of him, a razor-sharp yardstick measuring the distance for a killing strike. A split second later his hands moved in a blurring motion.

The Executioner waited until the sword strike was totally committed before going into action. Aware that the blade would cleave his skull if he tried the same maneuver as before—Kuro was too close to him to completely block the downward slash—the Executioner whipped the rifle straight up with his right hand.

Metal sang against metal as he deflected the sword off to the right.

Bolan stepped in with his left hand and stunned Kuro with a palm-heel strike to the shoulder. As the clansman lost his footing for a crucial split second, the warrior wheeled away from him, left hand gripping the rifle barrel, right hand going for the trigger.

He dropped back to the ground, his elbow jamming into the earth, the sniper rifle slanting upward like a planted flag.

Kuro made a final, desperate move to save himself. His right hand snapped out from his side, accompanied by the whisper of the sword cutting the air.

Bolan pulled the trigger.

The customized sound suppressor of the sniper rifle reduced the sharp crack of the 7.62 mm bullet that hit Kuro in the chest. His forward momentum carried him through with his sword strike, but Bolan dodged to the left and the blade swung harmlessly past.

Kuro leaned forward on the sword, using it like a cane to take another step toward Bolan. There was a look of fire in his eyes as if somehow the Executioner had broken the rules and the wrong man had been killed, as if tradition demanded that Bolan stay immobile while the sword sliced into his head.

Kuro's head dropped, looking down at the ribbons of blood spreading over him. The man was a step away from death.

A dangerous place to be—for Bolan. Kuro had nothing left to lose. More corpse than warrior, he lunged forward, intent on taking Bolan with him. His sword cuffed through the snow in a slash toward the Executioner's groin, which would have killed him in half a minute.

If he hadn't broken Kuro's rules again.

Bolan parried the thrust with the rifle barrel, then slammed the stock into Kuro's jaw. The Japanese fell back onto the snow, unmoving, staring sightless toward the sky.

A gust of wind screeched overhead, a bitter howl escorting the soul away. The shrieking wind spiraled downward suddenly, scattering the snow at Kuro's feet as if it were seeping through the cracks of the earth and tugging him into the underworld.

Kuro had been no saint. Many innocent souls had preceded him on the journey he now was taking. Bolan was lucky. The man had managed to surprise him, almost fatally. He'd either happened to be out on patrol or had somehow been warned of the Executioner's presence.

Bolan's thoughts turned to the warmth of the cabin. He felt drained from the fight and from the long climb up the mountain. His body had finally reached the limits of endurance. He needed warmth, and not from the business end of a rifle. The guards who'd stood watch—but hadn't seen him—were now probably double-timing it to his position. Though the AIM L96A1 sniper rifle had a sound suppressor, the solitary shot was still loud enough to be heard.

They'd arrive soon.

He retrieved his pack and shook off the snow, then headed for the ruins, mists of breath preceding him in the bone-chilling air.

As he neared the remnants of the shrine, he felt as if he were stepping back through time into a neolithic camp of piled stones and wood. Maybe this was how it had been thousands of years ago when the first temples were built to different gods.

He passed through a triad of entrance gates that were little more than poles with eroding cross-beams. The gates led toward a small shrine that resembled a lean-to of crumbling wood, leached almost white by the elements.

A water basin at the front of the shrine was half-full of snow. Inside the shrine itself was a small altar piece, beside which stood a hinged wooden box with its lid open in a vertical position. It looked like a treasure chest and contained a pair of rolled-up black paper scrolls tied with delicate silk lace. Next to them was something much less traditional—a radio transceiver.

A fleeting smile crossed the Executioner's lips. Kuro had been communing with more than just the gods of the mountain. He'd also been keeping in touch with the guards. Had they warned him? Had he warned them that he'd be outside looking for an intruder?

Stepping closer, Bolan saw carefully etched lettering on the outside of the scroll. Two English characters, *U.P.*, were followed by Japanese characters.

That was the name of the clan, or the gods they followed, Bolan thought.

On closer examination he saw another kind of treasure on the bottom of the casket, a more tangible one this time. It was a technical manual, thick, bound and heavy, one of the bibles of the kinetic weaponry defense project that Kuro's clan had pirated.

Instead of reaching for the manual, Bolan stepped back to one of the outer gates of the shrine, toppled the thin wooden pillars and carried one back into the shrine. Using the long wood as a pole, he tipped the casket over onto its side.

There was no explosion, no spring-held blade shooting up from the casket bottom.

It wasn't booby-trapped, and he hadn't really expected it to be. But there was no sense in taking chances now that he'd gotten this far.

After searching the rest of the area, Bolan headed for the cabin.

With a light push the heavily braced door swung inward and rapped against the inside wall. A wave of heat rushed out into the frigid air, fueled by the steady crackling flame in the stone hearth.

Bolan scanned the interior, the barrel of the sniper rifle also seeking occupants.

It was deserted except for the wraith by the window.

He saw what had provided the silhouette he'd spied. A suit of lightweight wraparound armor was carefully propped up on a low table by the window. Lacquered leather and iron plates were woven together with thick lacing. The armor was positioned so the flickering light from the hearth cast a man-shaped shadow on the drawn shade.

The rest of the cabin was sparse, but it, too, had the feeling of a shrine, with long ink sketches hanging from the walls. Kuro had been an artist, as well as an assassin. The sketches looked primitive, almost shamanic.

Though he'd familiarized himself over time with Japanese culture and knew something of the sects and martial cults, Bolan wasn't all that familiar with the pantheon of gods hanging from the walls. They seemed illusory to him. The only god he'd expected to meet on the mountain was the god of war.

On a small shelf by the drawings was a colored ink portrait. It resembled Kuro somewhat, with the short black hair cut sharply, like an ax head resting on the temples. And there was the same steely look in his eyes.

It could have been Kuro's father, maybe a brother, or perhaps even an ancestor. There was another possibility that came to mind. The portrait could have been a dopplegänger, Kuro's psychic double or his familiar spirit.

The Executioner dismissed it for now. Such conjecture was for the Wonderland Trust, Hal Brognola's Justice Department fiefdom that was responsible for sending him here in the first place.

Now he had more-immediate concerns.

He crouched by the stone platform in front of the hearth, took off his soaking-wet fingerless gloves and warmed his hands by the coals. His fingers felt numb at first but quickly came back to tingling life.

He removed one of the outer shells of his winter whites, then checked out his rifle. The weapon had been banged up solidly in his fight with Kuro, but still worked properly.

His pack contained several 10-round magazines for the rifle, as well as clips for his Beretta 93-R. He'd also packed adequate survival gear such as rations and snowshoes—everything he needed for his return trip off the mountain.

This was the heart of the crime clan. A broken heart at that. And soon the mourners would come in force.

THEY CAME FOR HIM within the hour. Two groups of white-clad clansmen spread out along the mountain face. There were about twenty of them in all, and they were moving fast.

Kuro either hadn't responded to their calls, or they'd been alerted by the single rifle shot that had echoed through the crisp mountain air.

Bolan tracked them through the Schmidt and Bender telescopic sight on the sniper rifle, scoping a few American and European faces scattered among the gunmen.

The advance gunners moved like a cracking whip, one after the other springing forward, diving into the snow, then aiming their weapons toward the collection of buildings surrounding the shrine. The rear guard covered their approach until the first unit took position, then they followed suit.

The Executioner waited for them behind a two-foothigh wall, all that remained of one of the cabins to the left of the shrine. Buttressed with slabs of rock piled in front of the wood, it made a natural barricade.

His position gave him a clear line of fire down the mountainous approach. At the same time it removed him a safe distance from the cabin, where smoke still plumed from the chimney.

Bolan figured they'd try to reach the cabin to see if their leader was still alive. But there was always the chance they had instructions to destroy the structure under certain circumstances.

He waited as long as he could—until it was courting suicide to wait any longer.

The first half dozen men were less then fifty yards away, their white-cloaked profiles sprouting up like stalagmites.

He gauged their speed, their likely course of flight, and then exhaled softly. At the same time he squeezed the trigger.

The first crack of Bolan's sniper rifle took out a stocky figure who was gesturing to the others to follow him. And follow him they did as the Executioner triggered several more rapid-fire rounds, the sniper scope levering left and right, catching them in midscramble.

Automatic fire chopped the air as the guards returned fire. Their volleys chipped away at the cabin, chinking into the wood and drilling holes into the piles of stone littering the ground.

But they didn't locate the sharpshooter.

Bolan carefully picked off two more men who were standing waist deep in the snow.

The warrior emptied the first clip, changed magazines and continued strafing the clansmen. Like a lead buzz saw whirling down the mountainside, the deadly fusillade had a telling effect.

But so did the counterattack.

By now the enemy was firing wildly, directing gunfire at all of the structures on the mountaintop. Bullets ate into the stone barricade he'd set up outside the wall and nailed the already flimsy entrance gates to the shrine, toppling the crossbars into the snow.

Bolan moved off to his right, intent on using the DM-51 grenades he'd taken from his pack. Most of the rear guardsmen were clustered by the gray rocks the warrior had swept around on his way up to the shrine.

He gripped the first grenade, pressing the lever to its side while he pulled out the pin. Then he lobbed it over the rocks. A few seconds later a red-tinted snowburst erupted into the air. The blast sent both men and weapons flying.

Bolan tossed two more grenades, the thump and roar of the blasts producing deadly aftershocks. The ice-cold breath of the mountain hissed toward the men who'd been creeping up to the rocks for shelter. Their quarry was forgotten as they ran blindly, discarding their weapons in a mad dash for safety.

Like gauntlets of ice, the hands of snow caught them, picked them up, then dashed them down the mountainside. The avalanche crashed them against trees and rocks before finally discarding their bodies under mounds of snow.

While most of the remaining clansmen looked on in horror at the men swept away, a trio of gunmen dashed forward on Bolan's left flank, rapidly moving from cover to cover.

Bolan mentally urged the closest gunner to dart behind a clump of rocks that protected him from the cabin, but not from the warrior's present position.

As if he heard the Executioner's call, the clansman scurried behind the rocks, leveled his rifle toward the cabin—and then keeled over as Bolan squeezed off another round from the Accuracy International.

The surviving clansmen returned fire. This time bullets flew above Bolan's head, boring through the wood and digging furrows in the snow around him. He squeezed off two more shots, then moved back toward his barricade.

The attackers realized the best way to survive was to storm the peak. They came from all sides, perhaps a half dozen of them reaching the summit at the same time.

The warrior didn't panic when they rushed him. Aiming just ahead of the lead man, Bolan triggered a 7.62 mm blast that cored his skull and dropped his dead weight into the snow.

The Executioner lunged to his right, rolled, then came up firing, spraying the air around the attackers while they were still shooting at his previous position.

There was a guttural cry of woe, and another man dropped.

Bolan's movements were instinctual, as natural as breathing. He predicted the movements of his enemies, what they'd do for each of his actions, and then, like a martial chess player, he made his moves accordingly.

He peered over the far end of the barricade, sighted on a target and felled another clansman with a head shot. Then, after pulling the trigger again, he watched his rifle jerk away from him and fall into the snow.

A split second later his mind registered what had happened—a whining piece of metal had torn open a gulley of flesh on the back of his hand, the impact knocking free his rifle.

Then came the pain as the bloodred gap exposed raw tissue to the frigid air.

Though blood streamed down his left hand, it wasn't a crippling wound.

Ignoring the pain, Bolan unleathered the Beretta 93-R with his right hand. Loaded with a 15-round magazine, the 9 mm pistol with a built-in suppressor could fire single shots or 3-round bursts.

Heavy footsteps sounded behind him, accompanied by shards of crusty snow scattering on the iced terrain. Two of the clansmen had wound their way through the ruins.

Bolan rolled to his right a few inches ahead of a stream of subgun fire that stitched the wood at his feet. He snapped off a burst from the Beretta that put down the nearer gunman for good and forced the other to dive for cover.

Rather than present himself as a target to the other clansmen closing in on him, Bolan scrambled through the snow, firing on the run.

Just as the warrior reached the ruins of another cabin, he saw a tall clansman striding from the opposite direction like a killing mirror image, his white cloak flapping like the wings of some great beast. Instead of talons, he wielded a submachine gun.

Before the man realized he'd found his quarry, Bolan took him out of play with a 3-round burst. As the body thumped down in the snow, the Executioner stepped past him and crouched behind some crumbling wall boards stacked together like giant pieces of kindling.

Most martial artists shared the philosophy that no matter how good a warrior a man became, there was always someone better down the line. And that was the person you measured yourself against, the invisible enemy stalking the boundaries of your will.

Today the clansmen of Ieyasu Kuro had found such a man.

They had attacked a superior force. Not in numbers, but in ability. That knowledge chipped away at their willingness to attack.

The Executioner darted from behind the ruined pile of wood, reaching his pack before the others could pinpoint his location. He removed several more of the grenades, then tossed them in a half circle in front of him, the sequence of explosions catching the clansmen in the midst of their final charge.

The incendiary blasts rocked the mountaintop, illuminating the thunderstruck attackers while Bolan picked them off one by one until, en masse, they retreated down the snowbound incline.

The Executioner retrieved his sniper rifle, then peered through the scope to make sure the enemy had really left.

The mountainside was devoid of human life. For now, anyway.

Bolan gathered the scrolls and technical manual from the shrine, then, from the bullet-riddled cabin, took down the ink sketches and portrait that had been on Kuro's wall.

Stepping back outside, he scanned the area once again, his eyes sweeping over the domain of the dead.

Then he headed down the mountain toward the drop site, where the clansmen had initially hoped to receive ransom.

Instead of ransom, Kuro had met the wrath of the Executioner, who had paid in full the going rate for terrorists and tyrants the world over.

YUKIKO CURLED her finger around the trigger of her 7.65 mm New Nambu automatic, trying to sight the pistol on the swiftly moving commando who breezed through the trees in back of the secluded roadside cottage. But he never stayed long enough in one spot for her to properly aim the weapon.

Instead, he darted in and out of the trees, trading shots with the clansmen. And they always got the worst of the exchange. Many of them had fled, taking most of the cars and their courage with them.

She watched the American move like a man possessed, like one of the *kami* who'd come down from the mountain, a god of vengeance. If the man was as good as the others claimed, then she had no hope with him.

Her hand snaked back through the open window—without the gun. She'd dropped it into the one of the snowbanks that had piled up around the house.

Then, as she heard more shouts and more gunfire, she tore off the thermal sweater that had kept her warm during her turn on guard duty. Dropping her hands to the middle of her blouse, the woman pulled sharply. The buttons popped free and rolled across the floor.

With a practiced grip, she spirited the dagger from her boot, pressed the blade against the front of her brassiere and cut through the connecting strap. Then she shredded part of her blouse so it looked as if she'd struggled with her "captors."

After disposing of the dagger, she unbraided her coiled black hair and ran her long, glossy red fingernails through it, mussing it up until it was unkempt.

All that was missing were some bruises, some scratches and the fear of the gods shining in her eyes.

Watching the man in action, fear was easy enough to summon.

BOLAN SPIED THE GIRL running through the carnage, screaming like a banshee. He stopped in midstride and watched her lithe form flee through the trees. Friend or foe? he wondered, looking for any sign of weapon.

Then he continued his canvas of the secluded cottage. The safehouse, war house, had become more of a retreat than the clansmen intended. It was time to move on before the mountaintop massacre and the downhill skirmish attracted the authorities.

Though they were in a secluded region of Hokkaido on the heavily forested and mountainous northeast coast, the Japanese air force had a sophisticated electronic-intelligence-gathering base at Wakkanai on the northwest coast. The ELINT operation meant security units were in the area, as well as quick reaction police units from Hokkaido's Twelfth Prefecture.

It was only a matter of time before they were alerted to the skirmish.

Bolan had to be long gone by then, but he couldn't just leave the girl, especially if she was in some sort of trouble. Of course, she could *be* trouble if she was working in concert with the clan.

It was impossible to tell.

He dropped out of sight behind a picket line of trees braced with waist-high snowdrifts and circled back through the forest in the direction the girl had been running.

She looked like a panicked deer thrashing through the trees, jumping and falling, screaming and grunting with pain. The girl was in midair when Bolan revealed himself, a white shadow emerging from the trees.

He stepped in front of her and caught her by the shoulders. The momentum lifted her off her feet, causing her to shriek as Bolan spun her around.

"Easy," Bolan soothed.

The woman nodded and gasped for air. Even with fear haunting her eyes, she was a stunning woman. Her long mane of tousled hair gave her a certain look of wildness, and though she was petite, she was obviously shapely, her full breasts exposed to the bitter cold.

She pointed back toward the safehouse, then spoke in Japanese that was much too rapid for Bolan's limited grasp of the language. Still gripping her shoulders, he spoke quietly, asking her to try English.

She nodded, again pointing toward the house, and spoke in halting English. "Criminals...kidnap me and—" At a loss for the word, she pantomimed starting a car. Then she grabbed at her torn blouse. "Try to hurt, but you come...."

Bolan weighed her words. It was probable that the clansmen would use a stolen, untraceable car, and if they had a chance to take a beautiful woman at the same time to sweeten the hours of waiting, why not? It wouldn't be the first time.

"How many are left in the house?" Bolan asked.

"Gone."

"All of them?"

"Yes."

He wasn't about to take her word for it. Returning to the site, he checked out the surrounding woods before creeping toward the back of the house and slipping inside.

It was empty. Outside in the long gravel driveway were fresh tire tracks from the cars that had driven off.

Now that she was inside the empty house, the woman seemed more at ease. Although she seemed in no great hurry to cover herself, perhaps out of shock, she eventually fixed her clothing.

"Are you hurt?" he asked.

"No."

Bolan made sure that her car was still there, and that she was able to drive. Aware that the longer he stayed, the riskier his chances were of going undetected, Bolan ushered her back out into the cold. Though the police would probably arrive soon, there was a chance some of the clansmen might return. It was better for both of them to leave.

On her way to her car, the woman looked up at Bolan and said, "Thank you. You are a very fine man."

As he watched her drive off, the warrior couldn't help but think that something was a bit off, something he couldn't put his finger on.

He wasn't sure if he believed her story, but he had to give her the benefit of the doubt. It could be just a case of being at the wrong place at the wrong time. Or it could be something else altogether....

Bolan crossed the road and headed downhill through the rock-strewn forest toward the shoreline. When he was a half mile away, he stopped at a small rise with a clear view of the choppy waters of the Sea of Okhotsk and the Nemuro Strait.

Then he opened his pack and removed the Motorola satcom unit. Fixing it in the direction of a geosynchronous military satellite over the Pacific, he keypadded a two-word code—Striker Out.

He headed toward the shore, where a rickety but functional dock jutted into the water. Concealed in the trees, he waited for his pickup.

A short while later a fishing boat drifted to the end of the dock. The forty footer looked like any other of the thousand fishing boats that plied the waters off of Japan, as well as the Soviet-occupied Kuriles just north of Hokkaido.

The fishermen were actually "CIA sailors," agents in place who now and then went fishing for commandos.

Bolan glanced back inland where the clansmen had met their deaths, victims of his cold fury.

Though the Executioner had more souls on his conscience, he could carry the weight. There were no doubts about what he'd done. It was never easy, but it was always necessary. He was a man at war.

2

The 6920th Electronic Security Group at Misawa Air Base was one of the most well-known secret operations in Japan—well-known in the sense that the American presence was obviously very strong there, as evidenced by the massive antenna array and reflector screens that took up a few football-field length of space. It was secret in the sense that very few people really knew the capacity of the Intelligence-gathering operation headquartered there.

In addition to nearly one thousand Air Force personnel stationed at Misawa, both the Naval Security Group and the Army Intelligence and Security Command had a large number of technicians and analysts on-site. All three services contributed to the National Security Agency's monitoring operation of the Pacific Rim nations.

Situated on the northern coast of Honshu, three hundred and sixty miles northwest of Tokyo, the base monitored Soviet military and civilian communications, as well as signals from China and Korea. The resulting Intelligence was shared with Japan, England, Australia, Canada and New Zealand.

All in all it was a secure area that required Top Secret Umbra and a half-dozen other security clearances to get on some parts of the base.

That was one of the reasons Hal Brognola had selected it for his meeting with Bolan. The head Fed had come up from Tokyo, where he'd been ironing out some problems with JEICO—the Joint Economic Integration Company—an umbrella organization for the American and Japanese firms working together on defense projects.

JEICO positioned itself at the crossroads where military research fueled the development of civilian technology to provide the necessary hardware. Since both the U.S. and Japan had been working on similar projects related to their shared defense concerns, both governments pushed for a joint effort. The creation of JEICO avoided duplication of cost and effort, and in the long run would give both countries a share in the profits.

Though it cut down on economic warfare, it inspired covert maneuvers. Despite *perestroika* and *glasnost,* the Soviet Intelligence services were working overtime to buy or steal high technology. That in turn inspired groups like Kuro's to cut themselves in for a piece of the action.

And it required men like the Executioner to cut them out.

Which was another reason why Brognola chose the Misawa Air Base for their rendezvous. Only three hundred miles south of Bolan's exfiltration site on Hokkaido, it was a good halfway point.

At three in the afternoon while a steady spring rain drummed on the roof of a prefab building on the northern edge of the base, Mack Bolan sat inside a nondescript briefing room. Leaning on a small round table, his right hand curling around a ceramic mug, the big man sipped strong black coffee while he studied the pained look on Brognola's face.

He'd finished his briefing on the Hokkaido hit, filling Brognola in on the good, the bad and the dead. Though there had been a few minor snags, there was nothing to warrant the gloom that hung over his friend.

Since their fates had been linked together for years, through the sanctioned and unsanctioned covert wars, Bolan knew him as well as any man could. The big Fed rarely showed his emotions unless he was being backed into a corner.

Somehow he had a feeling that Brognola was about to make some extra room for him in that corner.

"I got bad news, Striker."

"I kind of guessed," Bolan replied.

"It shows?"

"Yeah. Sticks out for a mile."

"A kick in the teeth'll do that to a guy," Brognola said.

"Who's doing the kicking?"

"A man called Kuro."

Bolan cocked an eyebrow. "Look, Hal, maybe this clan believes in reincarnation and all that, but it's a damn sight early for him to come back from the dead. Last time I saw Kuro, he wasn't moving."

"Not Kuro," Brognola said. "At least not the one you took care of on Hokkaido."

"Who, then?"

"His brother," the big Fed told him.

"Makes sense." Bolan glanced at the portrait that he'd laid on the table next to the scrolls he'd taken from Ieyasu Kuro's cabin. His index finger came down squarely on the forehead of the man who was dressed in the same type of ceremonial armor that Ieyasu had kept at the cabin. "This isn't an exact likeness of the man I fought at the shrine. I thought it was a lack of artistry, but if it's Ieyasu Kuro's brother, that explains it."

Brognola nodded. He opened up his briefcase, leafed through a manila jacket, then slid a few photographs across the table. They were perfect matches of the man in the portrait. His hair was cut short and came to a point on his forehead. And there was a haughty gaze staring back from the glossy photo.

"His name is Taro Kuro, and we've learned a lot about him since you left. He's the leader of a small but powerful secret society called U.P. Kobudo. Part religious cult, part crime clan."

Bolan nodded. They'd known that Ieyasu Kuro was connected to a clan, but they hadn't known which one. The one thing they knew when Bolan went in was that Ieyasu Kuro was a killer and a thief.

"That explains the initials on the scroll," the warrior said. "What does U.P. stand for?"

"It stands for 'Unseen Powers.' And 'Kobudo' means martial arts or skill."

"Unseen Powers," Bolan said, testing out the name. "Are they supposed to be invisible?"

"No, the unseen powers are supposed to be mystical, supernatural abilities given directly to the clansmen by the gods."

"The *kami*," Bolan said, using the Shinto term for the pantheon of gods. "They're not the first to claim a direct pipeline to the gods, and they won't be the last. I'll tell you one thing, though—maybe I was just lucky and the gunmen on the mountain forgot to wear their magic hats that day—but they died just like everyone else."

"The problem is," Brognola said, "that they were only the beginning."

He began his briefing on the developments that had taken place while the Executioner was in action. Right after the fishing boat dropped Bolan off on Hokkaido to make his deadly catch, Brognola's counterpart in Japanese Intelligence put him on to the man who knew more about the societies than anyone else in Japan's covert community.

"Are we talking about some kind of scholar?" Bolan asked.

"Yeah. The best kind. He came upon his knowledge the hard way."

"How's that?"

"He used to be a member of the clan."

Bolan studied Brognola, sure that the man wouldn't take them onto thin ice. But at the same time he knew that many of the Japanese clans had infiltrated all levels of society. From street gangs right up to CEOs, they had powerful connections. Did the connections go all the way to the upper echelon of Intelligence? Bolan wondered. "Did our man graduate with honors?"

"No. Actually he defected while he was still in his teens. It happened right after the U.P.'s went to war against another sect and a number of innocent people were hurt. He left the group to join the Japanese Self-Defense Forces and then spent several years with the National Police Agency. Now he's a senior officer in the Security Bureau."

"Perfect position for a mole," Bolan said.

"Yeah, it is. But he's not a mole."

"How can you be sure?"

"Simple arithmetic," Brognola replied. "Two attempts were made on his life shortly after he left them. Next thing you know, two clansmen permanently disappeared. From then on a kind of truce evolved as the clan stayed out of his territory and he stayed out of theirs.''

''But now they're locking horns again.''

''Right. He's just been assigned to the JEICO project to handle things on the Japanese side.''

Bolan nodded. It was a very neat fit. Almost too neat. Most legends were. If this security man was legit, fine, he could work with him. But what if the man had been working on behalf of the clan all this time? And now here he was in charge of conducting operations *against* the clan.

''Something tells me I'm going to be meeting this man real soon,'' Bolan said.

''Good guess, Striker. It's already being set up. He can give you more of a lowdown on the clan, but for now let me finish filling you on what we know so far.''

Brognola capsulized his knowledge of U.P. Kobudo. The very name itself hinted at its nature. Like many other Japanese sects, it selected English words for the first part of its name to demonstrate its place in the modern world and combined this with a Japanese word that showed their allegiance to a particular tradition.

The ''unseen powers'' stemmed from ancient Shinto deities, though it wasn't quite clear how those powers could be obtained.

''Now I'll tell you why we've done so much digging into this cult,'' Brognola announced, sliding another manila jacket onto the tabletop. ''The morning after your hit on Ieyasu Kuro, the Unseen Powers demonstrated just how powerful they are and how much they know about JEICO and its operations.

"First they abducted an American engineer in broad daylight as he was leaving a restaurant. Within one hour his wallet and ID were sent to JEICO headquarters to prove that they had him. At the same time a Japanese research scientist was taken from his home in Tokyo. A man came to his door and told the servant he had an urgent message. When the scientist appeared, the man pulled a gun and calmly walked him to a waiting car. The scientist's personal effects were also delivered to headquarters."

"Hostages to make sure they get their payoff," Bolan suggested.

"Not exactly, Striker," he said. "So far we're lucky on that count. Both men have been released. Apparently the clan just wanted to show they had the ability to strike at any time."

"What *do* they want?" Bolan asked.

"This is where it gets rough." Worry lines creased the big Fed's brow. He shook his head from side to side as he opened up the folder and took out more photographs—photographs of Hal Brognola coming out of a Tokyo nightclub with several high officers of JEICO; photographs of Brognola's wife climbing into the family car back in the States.

Bolan tempered the anger that seared his gut. The Unseen Powers could see all the way into the heart of the American government, threatening not only workers on the JEICO project in Japan, but a key presidential adviser.

"Now they're coming after you."

Brognola nodded. "My family's been moved to a safehouse near D.C., watched over by a crack team of federal agents night and day."

He paused for a moment, then said, "It's not me I'm worried about. Though we're not taking any of their threats lightly, it's obvious the clan is after something else."

"What?"

"They want you, Mack. They want you bad." He reached into the manila jacket, took out a photocopy of an ink sketch and slid it across the table.

The image was unmistakable. It was a portrait of a tall American with short black hair and a weathered, craggy face. It was a portrait of the Executioner.

Bolan picked up the picture and studied it closely. It was almost like looking in the mirror. The artist had caught him well, had obviously somehow seen him up close and captured the steel in his eyes. The only one he could think of was someone he'd let slip through his fingers. He shook his head. "The Japanese woman. It had to have been her."

"Both of the temporary abductees were given copies of that picture when they were released," Brognola said. "And they were given the message that the clan wishes to avoid a slaughter and wants no more 'unnecessary' harm to come to the good people of JEICO.''

"In other words they're willing to leave the company alone for now—if they can have me. And *then* they'll make more demands on the company.''

"Right,'' Brognola agreed. "First they want blood. Yours. Then they'll go for the money. Unless you accept the challenge, the massacre will begin. Starting with the JEICO people, then our people back home.''

"What's the deal?''

"The deal is that you're a dead man if you agree to their terms.'' With a clinical detachment, Brognola laid out the situation as the clan saw it. Since Bolan had killed one of their leaders, it was up to the others to avenge his death. The champions of the clan challenged him to mortal combat. One after the other they would fight Bolan. No quarter would be given.

"One for all . . . and all against me.''

"It's a no-win situation,'' Brognola stated. "They'll keep coming after you with their best men. They'll try and get you to fight on their terms, their territory. The odds are stacked against you.''

"They always have been, Hal.'' Though they'd hoped for a surgical strike against Ieyasu Kuro, both he and Brognola had been in enough similar situations in the past to know there were always aftershocks.

"There's no other way,'' Bolan said. "They've proved they can reach pretty much anywhere they want. To prevent a bloodbath, we've got to take them all out. For now the only way to do that is for me to accept their challenge."

"But you can't go in there alone," Brognola protested. "Hell, I should be right at your side. Stay with all the way—"

Bolan cut him off with a wave of his hand. "I'll need you for logistics, someone to pull all the right levers and open the right doors. Liaise with the Japanese, coordinate Intelligence, transportation, weapons—keep the politicians off my heels. You take care of that end, and I'll take care of mine."

Brognola sighed. His eyes fell to the bandage on Bolan's left hand. "You hurt?"

"Hell, yeah," Bolan said. "Hurt, but not crippled."

The warrior's eyes drifted back over the table at the scrolls, at the Wanted poster and at the technical manual that he'd retrieved from the shrine. That was one of the most ironic parts of the whole situation. Though the text and schematics were treated with chemicals and colors that theoretically prevented it from being photocopied, the top secret JEICO manual was actually a bit of high-tech blindsiding. There *was* accurate information in there, of course, but it was also packed with disinformation and dead ends that would tie up an outsider for years. Only someone who knew the real work of JEICO could decipher what was good and what was bogus.

Even so, the point was lost on the clan. They'd wanted a ransom from JEICO and, to prove they were dead serious, they had killed the engineer who'd been carrying the manual.

Bolan picked up his likeness once again—and immediately he thought back to the woman he'd encountered at the base of the mountain. The poor petrified "victim" who'd suckered him had managed to get a clear enough look at his face to draw him so that everyone in the clan would know who to look for.

Even when he had her in his hands, something had been bothering him, something that his subconscious had been working on ever since it happened. Now he knew why the woman's face had looked so familiar. He'd seen her face before he even met her.

"At least we've got one break, Hal."

"What?"

"The woman," he said. "We can send out a few Wanted posters of our own."

"What are you getting at?"

He tapped the picture the woman had drawn of him and said, "This works both ways. Our counterparts in Japanese security should be able to get a line on her."

"You going to draw her from memory?" Hal said.

"No," Bolan said. "Better than that." He pushed aside his poster and unrolled one of the colored ink drawings that showed the ancient gods and ancestors of the Unseen Powers sect. And there, her face in the clouds swirling around a mountaintop, was a portrait of the woman who'd run into his arms. He tapped his finger on her face. "I'll go after the clansmen," he said, "and you start looking for the goddess. Someone in Intelligence should know who she is and where to find her."

"We'll give it a shot."

3

Robot city, Bolan thought, slipping his computer-coded card into the scanner slot mounted on the table beside the hotel bed. He pressed the soft-touch buttons on the keypad, first turning up the lights, then turning on the television set bolted to the floor on a lecternlike stand.

All of it would be charged to the card assigned to Rance Pollock, one of the cover identities the Justice Department had prepared for the Executioner in Tokyo.

The user-friendly hotel was as anonymous as it was automated. Except for the skeleton crew in the lobby that helped new guests cope with the computer check-in system, there were hardly any signs of hotel staff.

Most of the patrons were there just for brief stop-overs. It was a flexible arrangement that matched moods, charging a person for as few or as many of the amenities he or she ordered via card or keypad.

Though it seemed stark and almost dehumanized, the hotel had several advantages. Everything was literally at the guests' fingertips, and the concierge was a computer who couldn't be easily bribed to talk about the guests' comings and goings.

It was seven o'clock at night. Bolan had been sleeping for several hours, recuperating from his sojourn on Hokkaido. He stretched out on the bed, watching a bilingual news program for any mention of the Hokkaido hit. Nothing yet. So far Japanese security had kept the lid on.

He turned off the set, took a quick shower, and after dressing in black pullover, jeans and soft-soled shoes, he packed some of his gear in a lightweight travel bag. He ran the computer card through the scanner one more time to turn on the television set again. If by chance anyone *did* come nosing around outside the room, it would sound like someone was inside blissing out on *HDTV*.

He took the elevator ten floors down to the basement garage, climbed into the sedate black Toyota sedan waiting for him and drove up to street level, drifting into the sea of metal and chrome that swirled around the Ginza district at night.

A half hour later, after taking several detours, he arrived at Makoto Tamura's headquarters on the outskirts of Tokyo. It was a monolithic office building of tinted chrome and glass that mirrored a moonsplashed pond on the right side of the building. It was past nine, but there were still several late-model cars in the parking lot.

He parked the car, walked past a well-trimmed garden, then stepped into a subdued but elegant reception area. If someone walked into the area by mistake, it would look just like a typical, successful company. Very nice camouflage, Bolan thought, except for the security guard whose pin-striped suit didn't quite cover the bulge of his underarm holster. He was standing behind the receptionist's desk, pretending to be looking over some papers—rather than the American who'd walked in.

"I'm here to see Makoto Tamura." Bolan spoke to the receptionist, a slight young woman whose easy smile didn't quite mask the suspicion in her eyes.

"I see," she replied in flawless English. "And you are...?"

"Pollock," he said. "Rance Pollock."

Her eyes dropped the professional coldness. He'd said the magic words. "One moment. I'll let Mr. Tamura know that you're here."

She made the call, then spoke softly to the security guard.

"This way, Mr. Pollock," the man said, his wariness abating slightly as he stepped aside for Bolan.

As the warrior walked down the thin hallway behind the reception area, he felt the same sensation he'd felt dozens of times before. It always happened whenever he stepped inside the inner sanctum of a spook organization. He was among friends—sort of. Until proved otherwise, Intelligence men suspected everyone of everything.

He couldn't fault them. After all, he did the same.

LEAN AND SERENE, Bolan thought when he filled the open doorway of Makoto Tamura's office and looked in at the Japanese security chieftain.

Tamura had been deep in concentration, his steepled fingers resting on the bridge of his nose. But the moment he saw the Executioner, he stepped from behind his desk. Obviously long accustomed to dealing with Americans, he reached out his hand in welcome.

He looked somewhat monkish, the grayish hair at his temples bracing his receding hairline. But his solid grip belied his passive appearance.

After exchanging pleasantries, the two men headed for the center of the room, where Tamura's uncluttered desk sat like a command post. Bolan eased his long frame into the chair facing Tamura's desk and glanced around the room. It was wide with a high ceiling and had a long window that looked down upon the water below.

"Nice to see so much empty space for a change," Bolan said, glad to be away from the crowded chaos of Tokyo.

"Not quite empty," Tamura replied, gesturing around the sparse office. "It's filled with my thoughts." Then he tapped his forefinger gently against his head. "Most of my files are up here."

"Mind if I grab a few?" Bolan asked.

"Of course, but first let me ask you a question. What brings you here, Mr. Pollock?" He spoke the name as if it were chimerical, something plucked out of thin air and just as weightless. "What do you hope to accomplish?"

"I understand you're the man to see when it comes to U.P. Kobudo."

"Yes," Tamura said, his English tinged with a slight British accent. "Anyone who confronts the Unseen Powers would be wise to consult me. Or perhaps more appropriate, the *Book of the Dead*."

Bolan smiled slightly. "Send a copy to the U.P. They can make all the preparations they want. Me, I'll take whatever you can give me."

"Very well. At Mr. Brognola's request, I'll take you into my confidence. But first let me make my position clear. My people are already moving against the U.P. and we can't stand by while some American cowboy rides in with six-guns blazing."

"I use a Beretta."

A trace of a smile appeared on Tamura's face, responding to Bolan's humor, but it vanished quickly as he continued laying out the guidelines for Bolan's actions in Japan.

The Executioner was unfazed by the lecture. It was par for the course. He was operating on someone else's territory and was supposed to play by their rules. Even if Tamura wanted him to go in shooting, he'd still have to go through the motions.

"No argument," Bolan said when Tamura finished talking. "But there's still one problem. I have no choice and neither do you. Unless I go in there with six-guns blazing—or even just a cap gun—it doesn't matter. I have to go in. The clan wants me, and they'll kill as many people as they have to in order to get me. That's what we're dealing with."

Tamura clasped his hands together. He looked resigned to the situation. Whether he wanted the tall American or not was beside the point. U.P. Kobudo wanted him, and for the moment they were the ones making the rules.

"You're right," he said. "You do have to go in there. But to do that you'll need a guide. And some backup."

"That's why I came here."

Tamura nodded. "Our mutual friend, Mr. Brognola, appraised me of the events on Hokkaido. Or perhaps I should say your government's version of events. I find much of it hard to believe. It seems beyond the capacity of one man to accomplish so much."

Bolan shrugged. "I'm not out to convert you. I'm just here to do my job."

"You're here because I respect Harold Brognola and have found him to be an honorable man. We've worked well together in the past. If he says you're the best, I'll respect his judgment. But even so, even if you were able to wreak such havoc on Hokkaido, those clansmen were nothing compared to what you face now."

Tamura expanded on the briefing that Brognola had given the Executioner on U.P. Kobudo. His knowledge of their leaders, their methods and their strongholds was encyclopedic. He'd kept tabs on his former clansmen, knowing that sooner or later they'd clash.

"The sect believes it's on a sacred mission. Several of their clansmen are appointed as champions. These are their best warriors, and they're a different breed from Ieyasu Kuro. As dangerous as he was, Ieyasu was a master of deception, a killer and a schemer. But he wasn't one of their true champions. Their champions are considered to be adepts. These most devoted acolytes of Taro Kuro are mystic warriors who believe themselves in contact with—or possessed by—the spirits of their ancestors."

"Not an uncommon belief," Bolan observed.

"True. In most cases. In this case, however, the sect believes their ancestors were gods, and as gods they are above the law. In fact, they create their own laws."

Tamura explained that each of the sect's champions was responsible for enforcing the sect's laws in different provinces of Japan. The sect itself had grown strong over the years, infiltrating and controlling several legal, as well as underground, enterprises across the country.

"The Unseen Powers are making their move now. They've always considered themselves the true patriots of Japan and now they're trying to prove it to everyone else. But they are being very clever about it. Though Taro Kuro gives the orders, he's never been implicated in any of their crimes. He's too well-insulated from the criminal activities of his underlings. No clansmen will mention his name. And he tolerates no failures. Nor does he tolerate disloyalty."

"Like the Yakuza gangs?" Bolan suggested.

"More fanatic. Instead of cutting off a joint or two, they cut off the entire spirit. Death is the punishment for members who fail Kuro in any way. Of course, in Kuro's theology, this is a great favor. The member will be sent back to the land of spirits where he'll be given a chance to start all over again."

"Sounds like a thoughtful guy. Where can I find him?"

"He's always on the move. Though his main headquarters are on a small island off of Hokkaido, there are several other places he frequents. Rural retreats. City homes. He moves like the wind. Never in one place long enough for anyone to find him."

"I'll find him," Bolan vowed.

"How?"

"Simple," he said. "If Kuro is the leader of these mystic warriors they must see him as the ultimate champion. That means sooner or later he'll have to face me."

"If you live that long," Tamura said wryly. "But first you must defeat his champions, and that won't be easy. If you want to find Kuro, let me show you what you're in for."

The Japanese security man gestured toward the door and led Bolan out of the office to the elevator. They rode down to a subbasement level, where a maze of thin concrete corridors spiraled out from the elevator banks, making Bolan think of a rabbit warren.

They wound through several corridors and stopped before a pair of wide double doors that opened into a large gymnasium-style room. The wooden floor was polished to a glossy icelike finish.

Tatami mats lined one side of the room while an assortment of weaponry hung from racks along the opposite wall, ranging from wooden practice halberds and swords to police batons and trident-shaped *sais* that were used to block or break swords.

The battle room was spotless. Everything was in place, right down to the trays of *shurikens* that slanted out from the wall. Heavily weighted *makiwara* posts were worn smooth in spots from countless bare-knuckle punches. A man-shaped wooden silhouette stood about thirty feet away.

"Nice," Bolan commented, looking around the dojo. "Is this where I find Kuro?"

"In a way, yes. I wanted to demonstrate just how deadly Kuro's champions are." Tamura pointed toward the wooden silhouette and said, "For example, you'd have little chance of surviving an attack from one of their swordsmen, even though he was that far—"

Bolan spun to his left and grabbed a spear-shaped bolt with his right hand. He continued pivoting around in a blurlike motion. Changing his balance at the end of the maneuver, he shifted his weight forward onto his left foot as his right hand whipped air.

The iron bolt drilled the silhouette right in the middle of the head, splintering through the wood and echoing across the room.

"That far away?" Bolan asked, finishing what Tamura had been about to say.

Again the smile appeared, but only for a second. "Impressive," he said, "if a bit one-sided. After all, wooden soldiers are notoriously slow."

"I'm not trying to impress anyone. I just like to cut to the chase. If you need convincing before you steer me in the right direction, I'll convince you."

Tamura nodded. "I mean no reflection on your skills. I mean to show you how good these champions really are. Often you'll have to face them on their terms. Their weapons. Their territory. Yes?"

"Yes," Bolan agreed.

The security chief stepped over to the wall and took down two *bokkens*. The wooden training swords were just over three feet long, and though they were deceptively harmless in appearance, a practiced hand could kill a man with the hardwood weapon.

Tamura handed one of the swords to Bolan, giving him a chance to heft it and get used to the weight.

They bowed, circled each other, then clashed swords.

Bolan parried a downward slash, then swept the edge of his wooden blade for a cut to Tamura's knee. The Japanese jumped aside, spun and unleashed a whip-fast cut at Bolan's neck. The Executioner saw it coming, deflected it with a two-handed block and countered with a slash toward Tamura's throat.

They took each other's measure, gradually increasing the strength and velocity of their sword strikes. A steady clak-clak echoed in the room as sweat poured down each man's face, their shirts becoming soaked with perspiration.

They accelerated their combat until both men were slashing with almost full force.

Then both men suddenly stepped back.

"You have trained well, Rance," Tamura praised, using his first name for the first time. "More than just the tourist I expected."

"You're also an accomplished fighter, Makoto," Bolan replied. "Your teacher has much to be proud of."

Tamura shook his head. "Actually he'd be quite saddened if he saw me now. And most likely one of us would be quite dead. My teacher was Taro Kuro. He was the best swordsman in the sect. A natural warrior. If anyone could realize their outlandish claims, it would be him.''

''Do you believe he has unseen powers?''

''I'll believe them when I don't see them,'' Tamura said. His quick wide smile flashed a set of bright and even teeth—except for one of his upper middle teeth on the right. It had been severely chipped, perhaps from steady combat in this room, perhaps from more serious combat outside. It slanted down like a guillotine and gave him a somewhat predatory look, an image quite useful in his line of work.

Tamura took the swords, wiped them clean, then replaced them in the racks.

Then he looked at Bolan as if the two men had just met. ''You and I have a lot to discuss,'' he said. ''Many things I should tell you before you go off to find Kuro.''

''Thank you,'' the warrior replied, realizing they'd found common ground at last.

4

The Mazda AZ550 sports car drove east from Shinjuku Station and headed for Kabukicho, Tokyo's "Times Square" area, where the streets were full of neon and nylons.

Sex shops, nightclubs, blues bars and massage parlors lay in wait for tourists and Japanese businessmen who made up most of the after-hours clientele.

Many of the hot spots had bright neon signs or large lurid posters that proclaimed what was available inside like menus of sin. The clubs crowded one another on the narrow winding streets, some of them little more than subterranean walk downs, others looking like sleek but decadent clubs.

It was a permanent midnight Mardi Gras where anything could be had for a price. And like other places of its kind, the area had its own keepers.

The Yakuza clans had a strong presence in the area. So did U.P. Kobudo.

After a quick prowl of the bustling pleasure zone, the Mazda sports car screeched to a stop in front of Club Scandinavia. The driver loudly revved the en-

gine as he backed into the solitary parking space that
had been guarded by a couple of blue-jeaned, black-
jacketed toughs. They nearly jumped out of their
sharp-toed boots and scrambled onto the sidewalk.

One of them hurried inside the club; the other
glared at the tinted windows of the sports car.

Neon apparitions of dancers with exaggerated busts
flashed on and off from the Club Scandinavia sign
hovering above the sidewalk, the X-rated reflections
dancing all over the windshield and gleaming red roof
of the Mazda.

As the gull-wing doors swung open, Mack Bolan
stepped out from the passenger side. He looked down
at the black-jacketed hood, who suddenly appeared to
lose all interest in the car and its occupants.

Like a warrior who'd just reached Valhalla, Makoto Tamura slid out from the driver's seat and looked
up at the flickering dancers. Then he was looking up
into the face of a bullet-headed man who'd dashed out
from the club's doorway, bellowing a torrent of guttural threats at the new arrivals.

Tamuro smiled and spoke softly to the man. At the
same time he raised his hand with his palm outward.
That simple gesture soothed the savage beast.

At least for the moment.

Bullet Head stopped shouting, then looked into the
club to see how many of his compatriots had wit-
nessed the altercation. Finally he hurried back inside.

"What was that all about?" Bolan asked as they headed toward the entrance.

"The gentleman explained that the parking spot was reserved."

"And?"

"I thanked him for his consideration. It's so hard to find parking spots in Tokyo these days."

"That's all?"

Tamura cocked his head as if he suddenly remembered something. "There might have been something else."

"What?"

"Loosely translated, I said I'd rip off his head, drink out of his skull and feed the rest of his body to the fishes. By then he realized who I was and graciously permitted me to use the boss's parking space."

The two men pushed through the small but boisterous crowd of young toughs who'd filtered out to the street to see what had deflated Bullet Head. Like uniformed riffraff, they wore the same style blue jeans and black jackets.

"Good move," Bolan said when they passed the last of the apprentice gangsters and stepped into a small alcove shielded from the club by another set of glass doors. "No one will even notice we came here for a recon."

"This recon is for the clan. I want them to see what's coming for them on the horizon."

"Then you're batting a thousand so far," the warrior told him.

Loud thumping music boomed out through the seam of the doors as the band started another set.

Bolan looked through the glass and saw the familiar face of the underworld looking back—men and women on the make. Several well-dressed tourists and businessmen milled about, looking for a bit of wild life.

"Something tells me I'm not dressed right for the occasion," Bolan said.

"You're fine." Tamura inspected Bolan's garb. "No neckties required here."

"I was thinking more along the lines of something in basic black. Like a machine gun."

"Trust me."

"I guess I'll have to," Bolan replied. To him, the place had all the welcome of an armed camp—an enemy camp at that. A wrong move here could jeopardize his entire mission. But if Tamura figured the risks were worth it, Bolan would play along.

A barrage of blues hit them from huge monolithic speaker columns staggered around the club, making it look like an electronic Stonehenge. Blond hostesses swiveled their way around the columns, carrying trays of drinks for customers.

Tamura led the Executioner to the back of the club, where an empty table waited for them near the stage.

A hostess zeroed in on them, getting their drink orders before they even sat down.

To the staccato burst of a fuzz-toned blues guitar, a statuesque blonde clattered across the stage on high heels and stockings, just about all that remained of her costume. Floodlights blazed on her Pan-Caked flesh as she prowled along the edge of the stage.

For a split second Bolan thought he caught her exchanging a glance with Tamura, but then again, in a place like this it was her job to create the illusion that she shared secret passions with all of the men who watched.

The warrior scanned the crowd. All the hostesses were blond, many of them with the help of chemicals. Like most of the clubs in the area, it catered to certain tastes. And this was obviously the land of big-breasted blondes, nordic nirvana for those who could afford it.

Bolan curled his hand around one of the glasses of whiskey that the security chief had ordered for them. He raised it to his lips but didn't drink from it. As a matter of course, he assumed it could have been tampered with. But just as important, he wasn't about to cloud his judgment in case he had to go into action.

His eyes suddenly focused on a woman off to his right. The raven-haired woman was staring at him from a curtained corridor that led to the back rooms of the club. She wore a snug, night black dress and could have held her own with any of the dancers. He'd seen ample proof of that.

"There she is," Bolan said.

"Who?" Tamura turned to look, but by then she was gone. Only a splinter of light escaped from the narrow gap between the curtains rippling over the floor.

"The goddess."

"Unless you're talking about a fertility goddess, I wouldn't hope to find her here."

"I'm talking about the woman from the mountain, the one pictured in the scroll. The one who saw me on Hokkaido."

"You're right," Tamura said. "It is her." He leaned across the table and said, "Here name is Yukiko, and she has an interest in this club. She helps oversee some of the clan operations and sits at Kuro's right hand."

"You knew she operated out of here all along."

"I believed it was her," Tamura told him, "but I wanted to make sure. And now that you've identified her, we'll proceed from here."

"Take her into custody?"

Tamura shook his head. "A difficult proposition. We know she's as guilty as sin, but you're the only one who can place her on the mountain. Officially you weren't even there, as your testimony would be quite dubious. Not that we would ever want you to act as a witness."

"What, then?"

"As long as we don't arrest her, we can put the heat on Kuro whenever we want. In this case the threat of arrest is better than the act."

Bolan understood. Though she was a player, Yukiko could also be a pawn in the deadly game he and Tamura had to play against Kuro's sect.

"Enjoying your drinks?" The blond hostess reappeared suddenly at their table, proffering two more drinks. She tried hard to disguise it, but her Scandinavian accent had obviously come by way of Brooklyn.

Tamura glanced at their untouched drinks, politely accepting two more. "They're lovely to look at. As are you."

She blessed them with a bright, promising smile and set down the two drinks.

After she was gone, the Japanese outlined the clan's Tokyo operation. Club Scandinavia was like an embassy for Kuro's clan. It was the place where they dealt with many of their contacts in the business world and the underworld. Deals were cut here. And now and then, a few throats.

"If this is an embassy," Bolan said, "it must have its share of spies."

"Over the years we've managed to get some assets in Kuro's organization. Mostly trustworthy."

Bolan nodded toward the stage where the stripper had just finished her routine to a chorus of yells and whistles.

"Is she one of them?"

Tamura's eyes widened. "You detected something?"

"It was just a look, a quick flash in her eyes."

"Congratulations. Most men never would have noticed her eyes."

Bolan shrugged. He knew that Tamura hadn't brought him here just to scope out his assets in the organization, or even to identify Yukiko.

The main reason was a man named Akira Takahashi, who was Kuro's main champion in Tokyo. He managed Club Scandinavia and a number of other establishments controlled by the sect. It had been his reserved parking space in front of the club that the security chief had taken.

And now, as expected, Takahashi had arrived, no doubt summoned by Bullet Head.

Like an underworld regent, Takahashi moved through the club with a phalanx of well-dressed bodyguards at his side. Bullet Head hung close by in the background.

A hostess threading her way through the crowd with a tray of drinks stepped nimbly out of Takahashi's way. She carefully avoided his gaze, obviously well trained to see nothing at times like this.

At the same time a small group casually drifted toward the table. It was the blue-jean brigade. Without attracting any notice, they set up a screen between Bolan's table and the rest of the audience.

Now it was time for their leader to take center stage.

Takahashi marched toward them with the bearing of a man about to order a beheading or two.

In a dark blue suit, Takahashi was a foreboding presence. His thick brows were furrowed with anger, and his angular light-complexioned face looked hard, as if it had been hewn from ivory.

His eyes darted toward Tamura, first throwing hot coals his way, then trying to scorch Bolan with that same stare.

The Executioner met his gaze, regarded the man coolly.

For a moment Takahashi registered a shock of recognition, seeing himself on a landscape well traveled by the Executioner. It was the landscape of war, and it gave the champion an unsettling glimpse of the nature of the man who had felled Ieyasu Kuro and over a dozen others on Hokkaido.

He regained his composure quickly. "This is a private club," he said, speaking English with a heavy accent. He rested his hands on the edge of the table and leaned forward.

"No problem," Bolan said. "I've got an invitation right here." He slipped his left hand halfway inside his jacket.

"Hold it!" Takahashi ordered.

Even before the man finished speaking, two of the well-dressed men who'd accompanied him had opened their jackets, hands reaching for their weapons.

Bullet Head had also stepped forward, eager to redeem himself in the eyes of his superior.

"That's far enough." Takahashi glared at Bolan's offending hand. "I don't want to see a gun come out of there." He smiled then, satisfied that he was totally in control of the situation. After all, it was his kingdom.

"Don't worry," Bolan said. "There's no gun in my jacket. My gun's here." He glanced down and slowly removed his right hand from under the table, far enough so Takahashi could see that the Beretta 93-R was aimed right at him.

Then the Executioner slipped his left hand out of his jacket, holding a postcard between thumb and forefinger. "As I was saying, I've got an invitation. Recognize this?"

Takahashi stared impassively at the postcard.

It showed a pastoral view of a hot-springs inn in Hakone, the resort area nestled between the coast and the mountains sixty miles south of Tokyo's metropolitan sprawl. The hot springs pictured on the postcard were part of a quaint complex of pools and cottages run by Takahashi. That was his true home. His retreat. The city was just the place where he did business. But the springs was where his soul dwelled.

Scrawled across the back of the card were the words "Wish you were here."

The postcard had been sent to JEICO headquarters along with the sect's Wanted poster of Bolan. It had quickly found its way up the security chain to Makoto Tamura.

"That is another place entirely," Takahashi said. "A place where matters can be settled."

"Oh, I plan to go there," Bolan said, "but I wanted to deliver my answer to you in person. I accept the challenge of the Unseen Powers."

Takahashi's minions looked pleased. The tension level sank. There would be no war in the club tonight, and U.P. Kobudo wouldn't have to show its hand. The secret society could go on being secret.

Then Bolan tossed some gas on the dwindling fire. "But I still have to wonder what kind of champion rules a whorehouse," he commented. "Obviously someone made a mistake."

"You'll find out soon enough," Takahashi promised.

"Yes, I will." Bolan flicked the postcard. Slicing through the air, it caught the champion in the throat, then fluttered to the floor.

Anger surged through Takahashi, but he didn't want to deal any further with Bolan. Instead, he turned toward Tamura and snapped, "What is your part in this? What are you doing here? It was a matter of honor."

"That's why I'm here." Tamura pushed his chair away from the table and stood. "To make sure there are none of the usual U.P. tricks. Consider me a referee. Or better yet, a judge. And tell Kuro I'm thinking of him."

Tamura turned, and he and Bolan walked through the gauntlet of clansmen.

They passed unmolested to the front of the club, then climbed into Tamura's car and tore off into the night.

"I didn't expect us to go waltzing in there like that tonight," Bolan said.

"Neither did they. But it worked out fine. You gave them something to think about."

"Yeah. It worked this time. But give me more of a clue next time."

"We'll have much to celebrate," Tamura said. "If there is a next time."

MIST SHIELDED the hot springs that flowed through the gorge. Waterfalls ribboned down a series of sculptured tiers, producing a constant rushing sound as the water spread out into a wide pool.

Several wooden houses with curved eaves were stationed on both sides of the gorge, following the path of the water. Some were fair-sized lodges. Others, perched on splintery ridges that jutted over the ravine, were little more than huts.

As the ravine leveled out, man-made lagoons siphoned off the stream and collected it in pools where bathers could loll in the volcanic-tempered water just a few steps from the cottages.

Like many other spas in the Lake Hakone area, the hot-springs resort offered an elegant retreat. It also offered a sense of mystery. Along with the soothing view of misted waters running past their cottages, guests at the inn could look at Mount Fuji in the distance, its snowcapped peaks masked by clouds.

Since feudal times Hakone's special aura had attracted peasants and royalty alike, who considered the pocket of land nestled between the coastline and Mount Fuji a sacred region. It was a land still full of primitive forests and lakes, a land that closely guarded its secrets.

And that made it a natural habitat for Akira Takahashi. Though he spent much of his time conducting underworld business in Tokyo, his true home was in the Hakone resort.

Until recently the resort had been catering to a steady spring-season clientele. Now it was closed to the outside world.

The Executioner crouched among a jagged spine of rocks across from Takahashi's lodge. It was dark. The outside of the building was lit by lanterns, and the intricately designed Japanese window screens were lit up from within.

Voices carried in the night from the small group of men gathered around Kuro's champion. As the hours passed, the voices had grown louder, stoked with saki.

It reminded Bolan of different times, different wars. He'd faced different types of families going to the mattresses. But it was the same war in a way, the same forces he was up against.

Footsteps sounded lightly on the wooden bridge as one of the sentries crossed over the planks.

Bolan listened carefully to the cadence of the man's steps as he walked back and forth. It was a sound he'd come to know hour by hour, the man's slow and steady gait as much of a signature as a name scrawled across a page. He could just hear them above the sound of rushing water.

Same as before, the sentry stopped in the middle of the bridge on his last time across, placed his hands on the railing and looked down at the water. He scanned the forest on both sides of the stream, practically looking straight at Bolan. But he saw nothing.

The Executioner was in black, his face smeared with dark combat cosmetics.

He stood perfectly still, breathing slow and easy, totally at home in the forest he'd stalked these past few days. He knew the most vulnerable paths for ambushes and the most likely escape routes.

Though the hardmen had toughened up their defenses all around the camp, Bolan had sailed straight into their midst with mask, fins and lightweight closed-circuit scuba gear. At those moments where he had to scale the jagged walls of the ravine, he unfolded a four-pronged grappling hook.

Then he'd settled in for the duration. And tonight it would end, one way or the other.

The clansmen had settled into their usual routine, ready to protect their champion. The Executioner was about to make them earn their keep.

He knew their strengths and weaknesses, how they moved, how they thought, and thanks to Makoto Tamura, how much blood they had on their hands.

Stone killers all.

They had to be, to get into the inner circle of Akira Takahashi.

Several days had passed since Bolan had encountered Kuro's champion in Club Scandinavia. But even before the encounter with Takahashi, the Security Bureau's Intelligence apparatus had been miking and spiking the resort, posing as guests to learn the ins and outs of the area. Tamura's squad had used miniature bugs and borescope camera lenses to map out the hotsprings terrain and capture the clansmen on film.

By the time Tamura's men were ushered out of the resort along with the genuine guests, the secret society had precious few secrets left in Hakone.

They made it easier in a way. Bolan knew he faced no innocents tonight. No one was in the wrong place at the wrong time. They were looking for war, and tonight they'd find it.

And now the hunt began.

Footsteps receded from the bridge as the sentry walked back toward the lodge. As he stepped on the walkway, there was no motion from inside the lodge.

Conditioned to the sound of the sentry, no one came out to check on the sound of footsteps.

Bolan unzipped the watertight satchel and removed the cross harness of throwing stars. Like a priest putting on vestments, he draped it over his back. Waiting in their sheaths like the spiny armor of an ancient predator, the razor-sharp weapons were dull black.

Though the silent and deadly missiles would definitely come in handy, they weren't the only weapons the warrior carried this night.

The Executioner reached into the satchel for a few more items, then hefted the silenced Beretta 93-R, flicking the selector to machine-pistol mode.

Then he went off in search of the "gods."

The nearest clansmen were stationed in a bark-shingled lodge with a wraparound porch facing away from the bridge. With the cedar walls and the curved-eave design, it was a small-scale duplicate of Takahashi's lodge, as if the champion's private retreat had sired several other quarters for his men-at-war.

Glowing cigarette ends punctured the darkness. Two clansmen sat on the porch by a small, round table. Lulled by the sound of the water and the hours of waiting, they were killing time before it was their turn to go on duty.

The steady clinks of kiln-fired cups proved that they were working on their supply of saki, perhaps even the bottle of Scotch Whiskey that Bolan had spied earlier on the table.

That was one of the appeals of the Unseen Powers sect, Bolan knew. Alcohol and tobacco were forbidden. Unless you felt like having them. For the true adepts of the cult, sex was forbidden. Unless you felt it necessary for your progress. There were no specific gods to follow. Any god would do, because after all, each of the clansmen was considered to have godlike potential. Their bodies were havens for wandering warrior gods of the past.

Despite the mystical trappings, the clansmen practiced a religion of violence, and Takahashi was one of their high priests.

Bolan stepped softly on the moss that covered the rocks. Once he was sure of his footing, he climbed up onto the ridge, his shadow swallowed by the forest behind him.

Then he headed for the lodge.

Rounded slates of stone dotted the grass in a meandering path that led up to the porch steps. The warrior moved slowly, the silenced barrel of the Beretta moving in front of him like a dowsing rod.

A soft cry of surprise floated on the air as one of the clansmen spotted him.

The Beretta spoke then, its hushed voice whipping through the night and drilling the man's chest to the back of the chair. His cup fell to the table, then rolled onto the floor.

The second gunman was torn between shouting the alarm or trying to save his life by reaching for his

Nambu automatic. He went for the latter and accomplished neither.

Like one of their vengeful gods, Bolan merely turned slightly to his right and squeezed the trigger again. The man fell back against the wall, a 3-round burst his only benediction.

The clansman slumped to the floor.

Bolan climbed the steps to the porch and checked the hardmen for signs of life. Their eyes were as vacant as their souls. He lifted them back into their chairs, then slid the chairs against the table. If anyone saw them from a distance, it would look as though the men were in conversation.

Two down.

He scouted out the rest of the lodge, then examined the rest of the stronghold through a thin bamboo curtain at one of the darkened back windows.

Not all of the lodges were staffed with hardmen.

Takahashi had staggered his men throughout the complex. A half dozen were stationed on this side of the stream. One sentry patrolled the bridge and the main lodge where the rest of the clansmen waited with Takahashi.

Tough odds taken all at once. But by going house to house, Bolan could even out the risks.

He drifted along the edge of the forest, passing an empty lodge and coming up on a small cottage with a tiled roof. Closer to one of the waterfalls, his steps were muted as he slipped through the front door.

It was spare inside with a low table, a couple of cane chairs and a small desk by the window. A shirt and jacket hung from a rack on the wall, floating above a pair of boots like a disembodied spirit.

Bolan came to a standstill when he heard a change in the breathing patterns of the man in the back bedroom. The rasping breath suddenly halted.

Coming out of a deep sleep.

The Executioner crossed the threshold and looked inside, where the clansman was sprawled across a futon, one arm raised over his head as if it were shielding him from a bad dream.

The man woke suddenly, alerted perhaps by the shadow drifting across the room. His hand scrambled for the holstered automatic pistol by the bed.

The warrior lowered the barrel and triggered a single shot to the man's forehead.

The hardman jerked once, then dropped back down onto the futon and fell into a permanent sleep.

Bolan moved on.

Farther up the ravine, another clansman stepped out of his cabin and stepped into the Executioner's line of fire. He spun around and dropped face first into the grass. Bolan dragged the corpse to the shade of the cabin.

The last two men were awake. They were on edge, obviously suspecting that something was up. Perhaps it was the lack of voices drifting up from the lower cabins. Perhaps it was the slight sound caused by firing the suppressed Beretta. But they were alert, searching through the woods for an intruder.

They found him halfway down the path leading to the other cabins.

Bolan was lying flat on his back in a patch of undergrowth that jagged out onto the trail. He sprang into a sitting position and fired off two quick bursts left to right as both men passed.

Like falling trees, the clansmen thumped into the bushes, sinking without firing a shot.

The warrior clambered to his feet, grabbed a clip from his combat vest—and saw a seventh man. A man who wasn't supposed to be there.

The broad-chested clansman had the look of a man going for a hunt in the country, a man who'd just flushed a stag from the forest. He was just as surprised as Bolan, but with a 9 mm Nambu automatic in his hand, he had the advantage.

He waved the pistol toward Bolan's hands. The Executioner threw down his weapon and raised his hands over his head.

His captor's eyes followed the weapon, a smile coming to his face.

In that split second, before the smug gunman could warn the others, Bolan's right hand dropped down the back of his shoulder, plucked a throwing star from its sheath and flung it.

The razor-sharp star buried itself in the clansman's forehead, a jagged stream of blood spouting from his cracked skull.

Even as the man's head was tilting back, Bolan's left hand fired another into his throat. It ripped into the soft gully of flesh, nearly coring his Adam's apple.

The warrior reached for another, but there was no more need.

The threat was gone, drifting away in a river of spilled blood.

Bolan replaced the weapon in its sheath, then pushed back the underbrush to retrieve his Beretta. He slapped home another magazine. Looking down at the fallen man who was making a rasping, gurgling sound, he ended the man's suffering with a single hushed mercy shot. Then he moved on.

His eyes scanned the forest and the lodges as he drew closer to the bridge, looking for more unexpected visitors. It appeared to be safe.

The sentry rounded the main lodge, heading for the bridge again.

Bolan had known the sentry wasn't the seventh man. He could tell by the man's girth. No, the seventh man had come from Takahashi's lodge. He'd either crossed over to this side to speak with one of the clansmen, or something had aroused his suspicion.

Whatever the reason, Bolan had to move fast. The sentry might be expecting the return of the seventh man any moment now.

Originally Bolan planned to ford the stream just below the bridge, climb up one of the brace beams, then take out the sentry from behind. He had to be up close to keep the man from making a sound. The numbers were falling fast.

The boards rumbled softly under the sentry's feet as he crossed the bridge to Bolan's side. Once he was across the bridge, the sentry paused in a small clearing and looked down toward the lodges, scanning them for any sign of trouble. There was none. Bolan had made sure the bodies were out of sight.

Besides, the sentry wasn't trying too hard. He wasn't really *looking*. He was acting more out of habit than out of a sense of duty, following the same patterns that he'd established throughout the night.

The Executioner understood the reason for the slack security. Much of it stemmed from their leader's attitude. Takahashi was expecting Bolan to march right into the camp and serve his head on a platter. Neither the champion nor the clansmen were expecting an attack.

After all, the American had accepted the challenge of the Unseen Powers.

Bolan had every intention of meeting that challenge, but on his terms. No one would know the hour of his coming.

Without the slightest inkling that his every step was watched, the sentry went back to the middle of the bridge and once more looked down into the water as if he were hypnotized by the rushing hot springs.

He made a perfect target in the splash of moonlight that lit up part of the bridge.

Not that Bolan would take a shot. Too much risk was involved. Even though the Beretta's sound suppressor greatly masked the fired round, the man could still cry out if he was hit, tipping off the clansmen in the lodge that something was up. Or the sound of his body falling on the boards might be enough to raise an alarm.

While Bolan was casting the man's fate, the sentry walked back over the bridge.

The Executioner started counting off, knowing exactly how long it would take the man to make a circuit of the lodge and return to the bridge.

The moment the sentry was out of sight, Bolan jogged across the clearing, slowing down when he came to the wooden slats of the bridge. He moved soundlessly across, looking straight ahead.

If by some chance the sentry came back ahead of time, he'd see the black-faced Executioner halfway across the bridge.

But the sentry kept to his routine, patrolling the far side of the lodge.

The warrior jumped off the wooden walkway from the bridge to the lodge, and he waited.

A few seconds later he heard the footsteps again.

Closer.

Closer.

The man passed by.

Bolan planted one foot on the walkway, then launched himself up. Creeping behind the sentry, he swung out his left hand, chopping the guy's trachea with a ridge-hand strike.

The man was stunned from the blow, unable to even gasp, unable to prevent his world from coming to an end as Bolan continued the maneuver, sliding his forearm around the man's neck and pulling back.

A weak kick struck at the warrior's knee, but the big man had anticipated the move, and the sentry's foot found nothing but air.

Bolan pressed hard with his right hand, pushing the man's head forward so his neck was caught hard in the forearm lock. With the oxygen to his brain cut off, the man slumped down.

Unconscious.

All along the Executioner had been backing down the walkway. Now he dropped to the ground with his burden. Pulling the man's hands behind his back, he looped nylon cord around them and pulled them taut.

Now it was time to meet Takahashi.

He walked to the side of the lodge and pressed his ear to the wall. The voices were steady and low, the voices of rulers, unaware that a usurper had crept into their kingdom.

Stepping around to the side of the lodge where a thin Japanese screen kept out the night breeze, Bolan unsheathed his combat knife. From the front pocket of his combat vest, he lifted an eight-ounce Hammer of Thor, a Haley & Weller E-182 multiburst stun grenade.

Bolan slashed up with his knife, cutting a gap in the bamboo screen, then he pulled the ring and armed the grenade. With a quick sideways thrust, he hurled it hard through the rent in the screen. As the grenade dropped to the floor in the center of the room, the warrior pivoted to his right.

The interior of the lodge went nova just as Bolan rolled around to the front. The flash-bang whited out the world for a precious few seconds, stunning the occupants of the room with a concussive blast.

While the clansmen reeled from the blinding flashes and the echoing roar of the grenade, Bolan ran to the front of the door, which opened just as he reached it. One of the clansmen had moved the moment the grenade was tossed. He came out gun first—but finished last. Bolan drilled him with a 3-round burst from the Beretta.

As the man slumped against the doorway, the warrior grabbed the collar of his shirt and yanked hard. The clansman crashed through the railing and onto the ground below.

Yells flooded the room as the disoriented clansmen staggered around in a daze, trying to recover their weapons and their wits.

Bolan jumped into the fray, knowing only one thing—of all the men in the room, he'd be the only one to walk out.

He scanned the room, his mind calculating how much time he had to deal with each man before they could turn the tables on him. Spinning to his left with a chest-high hook kick, Bolan planted the closest gunman into the wall. His huge bulk splintered through the delicate wood frame while his hands stretched outward, one of them wielding a gun. The warrior grabbed the barrel and smashed it across the man's nose, cracking cartilage and taking the guy out of the action.

Takahashi was on his feet at the far end of the room, looking on in amazement. One moment he'd been in control; now he was in the center of a deadly whirlwind dressed in black.

Bolan crouched and triggered a burst that kicked two more gunmen off their feet. Like a spray gun painting the clansmen with lead, the Beretta 93-R drew blood as it moved in a steady left-to-right motion.

The last clansman launched himself across the room, his right foot darting out in a sidekick toward Bolan's head. In a swift motion the Executioner closed with his opponent, foot forward, arm raised. He clenched his fist, turning his forearm into a ridge of stone that swooped up and caught the man's foot just past the ankle. Bolan continued raising his hand, pinwheeling the attacker down headfirst on the floor.

With a reflex move the warrior brought down his right heel hard, caving in the man's chest.

The gunmen of the inner circle were dead.

Only Takahashi was left alive in the room, and after seeing the Executioner in action, he had to suspect that it was only a temporary condition.

The black-robed, light-complexioned champion stepped forward, his face looking a bit whiter than usual. His eyes were glowing black coals that stared hard at the Executioner.

But looks didn't kill.

"You have violated the terms of the challenge," Takahashi accused, imperiously pointing at the silenced Beretta. "No guns. This was to be traditional combat."

"Yeah." Bolan glanced around at the fallen clansmen and the weapons that had dropped from their lifeless hands. "Those must be traditional automatics, handed down from generation to generation."

"These men were here to make sure our contest was honorable. They were here for..." He struggled with the right word in English, then said, "For insurance."

"Better get a new broker."

Takahashi's eyes met Bolan's, then dropped to the Beretta once again. "You endanger innocent lives. If the terms of the challenge are not properly met, war will come to the civilians."

"War will come to them anyway," Bolan said. He spoke softly, still holding the Beretta but not pointing it at Kuro's champion. "Your cult has fooled no one. Behind the mask of honor lies the heart of thieves and murderers. It would only be a matter of time before you returned to your true ways."

"You have already shown your true ways," Takahashi said. "Go ahead and shoot."

"No." Bolan harnessed the Beretta. "This isn't for you. It was for your hired killers. I'm a man of my word. You and I will fight with blades. Or hand to hand. Foot to foot. Whatever it takes."

Takahashi had recovered quickly from the effects of the flash-bang. Designed to cause disorientation for a number of seconds, the stun grenades caused no lasting damage. Bolan had trained with commandos who conditioned themselves to function even while flash-bangs were going off in their midst.

He strode across the floor and pushed open the front door, then called loudly to his men across the river. It was time to show them how a champion slew his enemies.

His shout hung heavy in the air.

"They won't be coming," Bolan said, stepping onto the porch behind him.

Takahashi laughed, knowing in only a few seconds they would respond to his yell. But the seconds passed and there was no response.

Kuro's champion stared long at the ravine, then turned to regard Bolan once again. He'd seen how quickly the man in black had dispatched the men in his lodge, and he realized that the men across the river had shared that same fate.

"Very well," Takahashi said. "You and I will have our combat. And I will tell the men of my clan that you fought honorably."

Bolan noticed that even now Takahashi refrained from naming Kuro, as if he'd be stricken dead for naming the earthbound deity of the Unseen Powers. Not a bad trick, he thought. No wonder Kuro had never been implicated in any of the clan's crimes.

"Unless you plan on coming back from the dead, Kuro won't know what happened here this day," Bolan said. "That's why I've kept one man alive to witness our combat."

While Takahashi searched for the surviving clansman, Bolan jumped from the walkway onto the grass. He lifted the man he'd choked into unconsciousness. Though a bit more force could have killed the man, Bolan had applied just the right amount of pressure so he'd only blacked out.

The warrior revived the sentry and yanked him back up onto the walkway, his hands still bound with the nylon cords. The man was startled but glad to be alive. For the moment, anyway. When Bolan pushed him back into the lodge after Takahashi, the revived clansman saw all of the guardians who'd fallen. His face paled as he staggered over to the side of the room where no bodies lay and sat down on the floor.

"Now we have a witness to tell the tale," Bolan announced, glancing at the Lazarus-like clansman who would serve as the referee. "Just like the bards of old." The Executioner removed his harnessed Beretta, slipped off his combat vest, then piled his gear in a neutral corner, far away from the bound sentry. Just in case.

"Now we must fight," Takahashi said.

"Yeah. But there is one alternative."

Takahashi arched an eyebrow.

"Kuro is behind all this. He calls for death, and I answer in kind." The Executioner glanced around the room at the carnage. "They didn't have to die. Not at my hand. Nor do you."

Takahashi's mocking smile widened as he waited for Bolan to continue, perhaps thinking that at last he'd found some weakness in the American.

"Sometimes words can be the sharpest weapon," Bolan said. "Tell us about Kuro, and the war will be stopped. No more blood has to be shed."

Takahashi sneered. "The clan has a way of dealing with traitors, a way we all believe in. If ever I betrayed them, they wouldn't have to send someone after me."

"Seppuku," Bolan said, referring to the ritual suicide chosen by a warrior.

"Yes."

"In that case let me help you along."

"*Hai,*" the champion said, bowing his head curtly.

Takahashi untied his sash and removed his robe, revealing only black pants and black, soft-soled shoes.

The Japanese was heavily muscled but not bulky. His body was lean and sinewy, trained for battle. There were no tattoos on his chest or arms, no missing joints that might have marked him as a clan member. The real mark of the Unseen Powers was much deeper—it was a mental scar that marked the disciples of the religion of violence.

Takahashi gestured toward a sword rack, a katana-*kake* that stood at the end of a narrow strip of unmatted floorboards gleaming with reflected lantern light. The killing floor.

The small rectangular sword rack resembled a pagoda without walls. The longer sides of the rack each held a pair of swords—katana on top, and shorter companion sword, the *wakizashi,* on the bottom. Their black-lacquered scabbards sported U.P. Kobudo characters etched in gold.

Takahashi offered one of the katanas to Bolan.

The Executioner unsheathed the long sword and studied the polished steel blade. Testing the sword grip, he turned the katana left and right in slow-motion cuts through the air. It felt a bit off to him, tainted steel.

"The swords are handmade for you," Bolan said.

Takahashi nodded, unsheathing his katana. It looked like an extension of his hand, a natural part of his being.

Bolan made a couple of downward cuts with the weapon, but he couldn't pinpoint the flaw in the sword. The weight seemed off balance, as if the blade weren't properly mounted onto the grip. There was an almost imperceptible shifting of steel as he tried a few more strokes.

He watched Takahashi move gracefully across the floor, the point of his sword etching intricate patterns in the air. No doubt the blade in Takahashi's hand was much better tempered. It would be steel versus twig if the Executioner went through with the match.

Aces and eights, Bolan thought. The champion had dealt him a dead man's hand. A man who could kill for profit, perhaps even pleasure, could easily push aside his honor long enough to give him a brittle sword.

Bolan held the sword in a two-handed grip in front of him, lining up the blade so it bisected the champion's face.

"Ready for combat?" Takahashi asked.

"That depends. If these swords were made for you, your spirit resides in them. Correct?"

Takahashi stared hard at Bolan. Like many sects, the Unseen Powers believed that the spirit of their warriors could be transferred to the steel of their swords.

"Yes," he finally said.

"All right, then." Bolan chopped the sword straight down into the floor. Splinters skidded at his feet. He bent the sword slightly and kicked out with his right heel. With a loud snap the sword broke in two...along with the spirit of Akira Takahashi.

The Executioner threw the broken hilt across the wood. "Now I'm ready."

"You have no weapon."

"I'll use this." The warrior unsheathed his combat knife, the blade looking like a metal toothpick compared to Takahashi's sword.

"You've made your choice," Takahashi said. "Now you must live by it or die by it."

Though the man's voice was low, it quavered with rage. Bolan had unsettled him. Insulted him. And unmasked him. Now, for his insolence, the American would die quickly.

The Executioner fanned the air in front of him with his left hand and drew back his right hand, cocking the knife by his side. Then he stepped forward, deliberately putting himself in the position where a trained swordsman could decapitate him with a quick two-handed stroke.

Takahashi's impassive gaze studied his neck as if there were a dotted line on it. One second, and it would be all over. The American would fall, and Kuro's champion would triumph.

It was too much to resist. Takahashi shouted, his *kiai* coming from a dark cavern within, sounding as if he were possessed by a feral beast.

The sword began its deadly arc.

But Bolan was no longer there. He'd watched Takahashi's eyes until he'd seen the other man commit himself. Then he went into action, diving to his right and swinging his right hand forward as if he were cracking a whip.

He released the knife in a quick snap.

The blade struck just under Takahashi's left armpit, burying itself to the hilt. The vulnerable spot had been unshielded for just that one brief moment when the swordsman raised both of his hands at the start of his swing.

Takahashi tilted back his head as the knife point cut through his heart, shredding his soul in that split second. For a moment he looked skyward as if seeking an entryway into the afterlife. But then he staggered forward, intent on finishing his sword strike.

Flat on his back, Bolan clambered out of the way. His hand shot straight up and caught Takahashi's wrist, turning it sharply. The long, curved blade chopped into the floor like a falling ax. And then, with a look of surprise carved onto his face, Takahashi flew past him and crashed to the floor.

Bolan got to his feet and looked down at the warrior whose reputation had long outlived his skills. For too long his underlings had done the dirty work while

Takahashi savored playing the role of champion. He'd become too attached to the pleasures of Club Scandinavia and the comforts of the hot springs.

The proof of that was buried in his chest.

The Executioner stepped forward, pressed his foot on the now-still body and pulled the knife free. He wiped the bloody blade on the dead man's black pants, then walked over to the sole survivor of Takahashi's crew.

Sitting with his hands tied behind him, the man shrank against the wall. Bolan crouched, spun him around and cut the cord.

The man stared at his freed hands.

Bolan gestured with the knife and said, "Tell Kuro I'll see him soon." He sheathed the knife, then walked out into the night.

5

Taro Kuro closed his eyes and watched the spirit world unfold. Takahashi bowed to him. Though the slain champion's image was ghostly, his face paler than a cloud, Takahashi's voice was strong. He spoke to Kuro in words and images an ordinary man could never fathom. He spoke the language of the dead and told Kuro of the demonic powers of the American who slew him. And he spoke of the treachery of one of their own former members, Makoto Tamura.

Then the rest of the clansmen who perished in the battle at Hakone paid Kuro their respects. Wearing fresh marks of combat like bloody red badges of loyalty, they made their apologies for dying before they completed their tasks.

Kuro nodded.

He understood. It was all part of the process, the path of perfection they followed. The American was obviously controlled by vengeful deities trying to deny Kuro his place in the celestial hierarchy. Vengeful, yes. Invincible, no. It could work both ways. The American could be a fire that consumed them or forged them into steel. That much was obvious to a man who knew how to look beyond the veil, a man who spent his life learning to be a god.

Then there was the matter of Makoto Tamura. Mako had turned against the Unseen Powers and summoned the American. He had betrayed the secrets of the sect to both the Japanese and the American Intelligence networks.

For that, Mako would have to die.

And the American would have to die.

That would end the curse that had fallen onto Kuro's house. Only then would Kuro free Takahashi and the others to continue their journey. Until that time their spirits were chained to him, unseen soldiers in an unseen war.

A sound crept into Kuro's consciousness. It was the sound of footsteps. Bare footsteps. It was the sound of a goddess approaching.

Without hinting that he was aware of her presence, he savored every second as she swept through the room, her robe swishing as it floated just inches off the floor. She paused by the wall-length window that looked out at the ocean that swallowed the lower reaches of their island.

To the rest of the world the small island several miles off the eastern coast of Hokkaido was known as Yamishima, mountainous island. But to the initiates of U.P. Kobudo, it was known as Kamishima, isle of the gods.

The god currently in residence was Taro Kuro, and the goddess was Yukiko.

He could feel her gaze shift to him. Her eyes singed his skin, hot with desire. Her robe shadowed the floor, then dropped in a silken hiss onto the bare wood next to the sunken bath.

The goddess was naked.

Her foot pierced swirling water, the soft splash rippling through his mind and tugging hard at him.

She called his name, but Kuro looked straight ahead, still watching the ghostly landscape that Takahashi scouted for him. And he walked alongside Takahashi's spirit, searching for the American. Finally he found him. The tall man was standing in a pocket of darkness, a cloak of death that followed him wherever he went.

Kuro recoiled.

He hadn't expected to find such a strong image. It seemed as if the black-clad phantom in his mind was looking back at him, meeting his ghostly gaze.

What manner of man was this? Kuro wondered. Was he like Kuro himself? More than a man? The Unseen Powers clan considered Kuro a *shugensha,* a magician capable of awesome feats of strength from both mind and body. A past master of mental arts, as well as martial.

Perhaps this American was also an adept, Kuro thought. After all, he had readily accepted the challenge to combat.

A singing voice intruded on his thoughts. Yukiko splashed in her bath, taunting him to join her.

Not yet, he thought, banishing all images of her from his mind. First he had to deal with the phantom that Takahashi had located for him.

Kuro struck out at him with the most potent weapon of all. His mind. He focused all of his being into one lightning-bolt strike. A brilliant flash coming down from the sky, searing the fabric of night and chopping through the American like an ax through a tree.

But the phantom American was unharmed. The image changed suddenly, turning into a death's-head image that grinned at Kuro before floating away into the dark streams of his mind.

Kuro's eyes snapped open.

The phantom had evaded his attack. In fact, he had mocked it, as if he were the true magician and Kuro the novice.

He quieted his heart, breathing deeply, taking air into his abdomen and coursing it through the cavern of his body. When he was calm once again, he closed his eyes and hunted for more prey.

Mako Tamura.

Mako was a recurring wound in his psychic armor, a cut that opened every time Kuro thought back to their early days together. At one time he and Mako were closer than brothers, closer than he and Ieyasu ever had been.

But Mako had severed all contact with the cult and turned against him. Kuro never forgot the day it happened. The clan was fighting a rival gang for encroaching on their territory. Mako, too, had fought, but he didn't kill. And he prevented other members of the sect from delivering fatal blows to their rivals. Even so, Kuro and some of the others had killed a man that day, a boy actually, still in his teens. Other skulls were broken, and other spirits flew.

After the battle Mako started walking and never stopped. He pretended not to hear Kuro's voice calling after him, a call that still echoed inside Kuro's head.

No defectors had ever been tolerated before. The Unseen Powers sent two of its strongest members after Mako.

The first one died with a broken neck and a crushed windpipe. The second had been found with his own dagger in his chest.

From then on the quest for vengeance had been postponed. But now there was no other choice. Mako was out to destroy the Unseen Powers, and Kuro would have to destroy him.

Kuro summoned an image of Mako Tamura and tried to strike him with his mind, just as he'd tried with the American. But Mako's image changed suddenly. Instead of an armed traitor, Kuro saw the young man who matched swords with him in the battle house, the only man he ever called his friend, the only one who could ever fight him to a draw.

Everyone else in Kuro's life had been a follower or a leader. But Mako had been an equal, at one time someone he would have died for, at one time someone who would have died for him.

That time was past. And now one of them would die at the other's hand.

Kuro came out of his trance, realizing that Yukiko had been talking to him. Her voice had become just a part of the atmosphere, but now he concentrated on her presence.

Still kneeling, Kuro turned toward her and smiled. His jet-black hair was freshly cut, honed rather, so it came to a spear point tapered at his forehead. It gave the impression that his entire body was a weapon, an image backed up by hardened muscle.

He regarded her as though it were the first time he'd set eyes on her nakedness. She was a water nymph, her lush curves shimmering in the steaming sulfurous bath, her skin rippling like a mirage. Her wet black hair framed her almond eyes and high cheekbones. It was a face that came to men in dreams, but came to Kuro in his waking life.

Yukiko returned the smile. "The American must be stopped," she said, "or he'll bring everything down around us."

"It's being attended to."

"Akira Takahashi attended to him, and what happened to him? Where is he now?"

"He communicates with me," Kuro replied.

"He lives only in your mind," she retorted. "A figment of your mad imagination."

"He lives," Kuro insisted.

"Tell him to bring me a glass of wine," she said. "When I taste it, I'll know he exists."

Kuro laughed. No one else could talk to him in such a manner, and that was one of the reasons why he needed her. He needed someone around to bring him down to earth, someone not afraid to throw a rope ladder to the clouds and pull him down.

"There are other champions," Kuro said. "Each has reached a higher plateau. They'll take care of the American."

"Oh?" she taunted. "I think the American will come to this plateau."

"I see," Kuro said. "What do you suggest?"

"I suggest you join me right now, before the water cools."

"What do you suggest about the American?" he asked.

"Champions are fine. As one course of attack. I think we should do something else to guarantee that he dies soon—before there are no champions left."

"No," Kuro said, knifing the air with his hand. "We have made it a point of honor that the American face our challenge in ritual combat. There's no other way we can attack him."

"Are the gods so limited they can conceive of nothing else? There are plenty of groups out there who would jump at the chance to work for you. We can't help it if outsiders end his life."

Kuro nodded, then looked down at her as she lifted her foot out of the bath, a sheet of water cascading down her shapely leg. "You have all the answers," he said. "Why not just kill me and take the reins?"

"If you wish," she said. Then she shrugged. The slight motion had an intriguing effect as her breasts peaked out of the water. "Join me now, and you can have a thousand little deaths."

The birth and death of pleasure, he thought. With Yukiko it would have many incarnations. He stripped and dropped into the water.

FROM A DISTANCE Kuro's sprawling headquarters looked like a shrine, but up close his allegiance to the modern world was as clear as the glass-walled aerie that capped the mountaintop estate.

It had a curved roof with upturned eaves, but rather than plain material, the roof was trimmed with onyx that matched the spires of iconlike statues gracing the outside of the building like futuristic sentries.

It was definitely a shrine, but it was a shrine devoted to the power and majesty of Taro Kuro.

Though there were a number of more traditional wooden and tiled buildings scattered through the forested slopes of Yamishima, this high-tech heart was the base of Kuro's operations.

The heavily forested slope leading to Kuro's home was dotted with terraced gardens and rustic buildings carved from the woods, occupied by the chieftain's most trusted retainers.

The only other approach to Kuro's retreat was a sheer drop that plunged down to a small fishing village below. Most of the villagers had been connected to the sect for years.

It was a safe haven.

Situated on the small mountaintop aerie was a sprawling estate that looked feudal on the outside, but inside had a wide variety of habitats.

Toward the front of the building was a large, modernized office that looked bare, until embedded computer screens were revealed at the soft touch of a button on the contoured console. A sophisticated communications network connected Kuro to other headquarters of the sect scattered throughout Japan.

Though many of the clan's practices were based on ancient beliefs, Kuro also had modern concerns. Many of the sect's younger warriors were in the corporate battlefield, infiltrating banks, trading companies and high-tech research firms. They offered a steady stream of insider tips and sensitive information on corporate officials who could be bribed or extorted.

These "zaitek" soldiers, modern corporate marauders, were just as loyal as the regular warriors. Kuro had sponsored their education and their training, furthering their careers at every step. And though the sect's fortunes were buttressed by traditional underworld enterprises like prostitution and drugs, there would come a time when the sect's holdings would be strictly legal. And then Taro Kuro would try to take his rightful place in society.

But first he'd have to overcome the man who studied him from afar.

SITTING IN A BRIGHT office at Tamura's Security Bureau headquarters, Bolan scanned the Intel on Kuro's operation. He grabbed the joystick on the videotape controller and fast-forwarded the film with a slight push to the right. Kuro's headquarters shot past on the television screen in a blur. He paused the film when it showed the main approach past Kuro's retrainers and up to his main estate.

Tamura had assembled the footage of Kuro's Yamishima fortress from a combination of overflight film from the Japanese air force, blueprints from the company that designed and installed communications equipment and up-close photography from assets that

Kuro managed to place on the island from time to time.

Bolan had spent hours going over the lay of the land, reading through the dossiers on Kuro's clansmen and memorizing their faces.

He studied the clansmen in the corporate sector, as well as the hard-core warriors Kuro claimed as his champions. The Executioner would soon be fighting them on both fronts.

Though he was tempted to launch a preemptive strike on Kuro's headquarters right now, Bolan knew that it would cost far too many lives. The clan was operating on automatic pilot. Unless the Executioner continued to meet their champions in combat, they would prey on the JEICO civilians.

No, he had to work his way up through the covert killers of U.P. Kobudo.

And then he'd pay his last respects to Taro Kuro.

6

Club Scandinavia was under new management. In the language of Kuro's cult, the former owner had transcended the material world.

The man who had helped him do the transcending walked into the club near midnight. He pushed through the throng of businessmen gathered near the bar and headed toward a small table at the back.

His regular table.

These past few nights Bolan had become a familiar sight in the nightclub. It was neutral ground. At least on the surface.

Using a number of cutouts, members of Kuro's clan had passed the word to Tamura that the club was a safe harbor where Bolan could pick up his marching orders. The Unseen Powers were in the process of selecting the next champion. When they chose him, the American would be the first to know.

It was a trap, of course. That much was obvious. The clan was simply making it possible for their outside gunners to get a good look at their target. Club

Scandinavia was neutral ground, so the hit would come somewhere else.

In the meantime Bolan watched the steady succession of grim faces float through the club, most of them looking at him rather than any of the dancers.

Assassins on parade, he thought. But it worked both ways. The warrior had a chance to scope out the hired killers the clan had brought in—as did Tamura's Security Bureau operatives who were sprinkled among the businessmen, grateful for the steady change of topless scenery. The security chief had brought in his best men to shadow the gunmen who were after Bolan.

The patrons barely noticed any changes in the operation of the club. There were still plenty of Nordic beauties patrolling the stage and snaring the customers.

And one of the favorites was still the tall blond dancer who worked for Tamura. She was the one who had overheard the details of the assassination plot.

Yukiko had come in to take control of the club for the time being, bringing with her a group of new faces. When they looked at the blonde, all they saw was a working girl, thinking she understood only bedroom and barroom Japanese.

But the woman understood what was going on, picking up enough information to let Tamura know when the attempt was coming.

Tonight was the night.

The hired guns thought they knew everything they needed to know about their mark. Bolan intentionally followed the same routine every night after leaving the club. They'd made a number of practice runs already, their car slowing down as it patrolled the street behind Bolan, lingering just long enough for a hit to be carried out.

Tonight they would try to make it good.

Bolan ordered a drink, but didn't touch it. He watched the dancers, but didn't really see them. He played the role of a bored American, a man who would soon be bored to death.

NIGHTTIME CROWDS FLOWED through the Kabukicho district in waves. Sometimes the streets were thick with staggering businessmen and their underworld shadows. Harsh feminine laughter echoed in the streets as the hookers lifted the spirits and then the wallets of their groggy customers.

Other times the area would suddenly fall quiet, deserted until one of the motorcycle gangs, the *bosozuku,* prowled the streets on their souped-up cycles.

Bolan walked along, watching his reflection in the storefront windows, as well as the skidding reflections of the nighttime traffic. Then he turned down a winding side street that was a jumble of shops, restaurants and hivelike apartment buildings, many of them shuttered against the cool night breeze and the thieves who plagued this part of the city.

A couple of times some street toughs stepped out from shaded doorways—then jumped back when they saw the Executioner's graveyard eyes staring back at them.

He was dressed for night work. Beneath his unzipped black jacket he wore snug-fitting body armor, the thin ceramic plates molded to his body. He was carrying a silenced Beretta 93-R in a breakaway sling around his chest.

Bolan strode past a tight string of parked cars, keeping his eyes straight ahead. But his peripheral vision picked up a man who'd stepped out of a parked car on the other side of the street about ten vehicles ahead. The man was decked out in studded black leathers, and his hair was cut short except for a lacquered lock that coiled down over his forehead. A Tokyo version of James Dean.

The Executioner knew that the Hollywood hoodlum was playing out one of his favorite roles. In fact, Bolan had seen him more than once when the gunman had come to Club Scandinavia for the underworld casting call.

The only kind of shooting he had in mind would come from the business end of the weapon concealed beneath the jacket slung over his arm. To a man like Bolan it was a bit obvious. But a midnight massacre never called for much subtlety.

James Dean started to cross the street, taking long strides while he stared hard at his target. He did everything but break into a wide grin, so sure was he of the outcome. Bolan knew the type. Dangerous but not a real pro. It was one thing to gun down an innocent civilian and get away with it. It was another thing entirely to go against a soldier of the night.

Someone revved an engine, and the backup car slowly turned the corner, coming up slowly behind the hit man.

It was a classic maneuver.

The hitter would come head-on, empty his weapon, then climb into the getaway car. If by some chance the hitter didn't make it, then the gunmen in the backup car would finish the job.

Classic, yeah.

But Bolan never went by the textbook.

The gunman flung off his jacket like a matador and stepped forward with his automatic knifing the air in front of him, firing off a trio of shots at his target. Only Bolan was already in motion.

The warrior had dived sideways a split second before the gunman made his move, reading the tension in the man's jerky movements. He ripped the Beretta free from its sling and triggered a 3-round burst that stitched a perfect triangle over James Dean's heart.

At the same time another shot from across the street cored the man's temple, kicking him sideways.

He was dead twice over and dropped heavily to the ground, a rebel without a cause or a breath to his name.

The Executioner's shoulder hit the ground at the end of his dive, then his legs went airborne and pinwheeled in the air. He came down hard on his feet, continued the roll and then scrambled into one of the narrow alleyways that splintered the block.

The backup car screeched to a stop.

"THREE MORE GUNNERS in the black four-door behind you."

Tamura's voice rang clearly in the miniature fleshtone receiver in Bolan's left ear. From his vantage point across the street in a third-floor apartment commandeered by the Security Bureau, Tamura had been able to keep Bolan appraised every step of the way.

The receiver was the size and shape of a hearing aid, and the transmitter was a miniaturized mike wound through the collar of Bolan's jacket.

"Got them," Bolan said to his invisible ally as the Toyota sedan gunned forward. It screeched to a stop at a sharp angle, with the passenger side facing Bolan. "You take the driver."

Like wings unfolding, the doors flipped open and the clansmen's hired killers spilled out, using the doors as shields while they sought out the Executioner.

Pressing the Beretta 93-R's extension stock against his shoulder, Bolan tracked the gunmen with the barrel. He zipped the first man head-on with a 3-round burst, the silenced volley spilling the guy back into the front seat of the car, practically dropping him onto the driver's lap.

At the same time, Tamura fired two rounds into the driver's window, pocking the bullet-proof glass and stunning the driver.

Two gunners were out in the street now, intent on finishing off their quarry. One carried a shotgun, the other a Japanese Type 100 submachine gun with a shortened stock. The man with the SMG, a long-haired broad-shouldered giant, vainly looked for Bolan, whipping the barrel of the subgun from left to right in his desperate search for his target.

But the frantic movements did nothing but stoke his own panic. The longer it took to make the hit, the greater the risk to the assassin.

He raced halfway to the alley and triggered a wild burst from the 30-round magazine. The full-auto barrage drilled into the brick walls like a jackhammer and sent a rain of dust and pulverized stone into the mouth of the alley.

But the target was still alive, and the gunman was having second thoughts as a rifle shot sliced the air just over his head. In his pursuit of a quick kill, he'd stepped into a deadly cross fire.

His prey was hitting back.

Bolan stepped out into the open and coolly took aim at his attacker, who lurched to his right and tried to line up the subgun on the Executioner.

Bolan shot from the hip and drilled the stocky gunman in the chest and head. Practically bursting apart at the seams, the would-be killer landed in a bloody heap, his outstretched arms reaching for the car.

The shotgunner took one step back and caught a slug from Tamura's sniper rifle, blood and bone exploding from the man's shoulder. He spun around and dived back through the open door of the back seat.

Running parallel to the car, Bolan raked the passenger side with a quick burst. The wounded gunman was screaming at the driver from the back seat while he tried to ward off the Executioner, waving the shotgun barrel around as if it were a magic wand. Then with a loud cry he fell out of sight.

With a crunch of gears, the driver backed into the street and into the path of an oncoming Mercedes sedan. A loud metallic thump echoed down the street as the blunt-nosed sedan pushed the getaway car sideways.

An alcohol-soaked driver in a rumpled blue suit came roaring out of the vehicle, bellowing at the battered getaway car he'd just broadsided. He stopped in his tracks, suddenly sobered by the sight of the automatic weapons and bloodied bodies in the street.

He ran back past his car and into the storefront shadows where stunned bar-crawlers had taken refuge, simultaneously attracted and frightened by the gunfire.

Bolan rolled across the hood of the getaway car and landed feetfirst on the road. He aimed the Beretta at the man behind the wheel, who was sat dazed by the crash.

"Freeze!" Bolan shouted. The man yelled something in rapid-fire Japanese, but it was clear that he understood the universal language of the Beretta 93-R.

The Executioner motioned him out of the car.

The guy raised his hands and slid across the seat. Like a sleepwalker he scrambled halfway out of the car.

Before the driver could even take one full step toward his captor, there was a huge blast from the back seat. The left side of the man's temple disintegrated, a piece of skull catapulting forward onto the street.

Whether the shot was intended for Bolan or the driver was a question that would forever remain unanswered. The Executioner jumped to the side and triggered a 3-round burst into the back seat. Though they'd hoped to take one of the gunmen alive, the warrior wasn't about to risk his life in exchange for a wounded prisoner.

The burst chopped into the man's head and heart, and drilled him back against the seat cushion like a trio of heavy metal studs.

Bolan stepped away from the death car. He surveyed the carnage, then looked up and down the sidewalk to make sure there were no more gunmen willing to try their hand.

The street was a momentary canyon of silence as those who'd ducked for cover realized it was over. Then, like a spring thaw had passed over them, they came back to life. One by one the shadows peeled away from the darkness. Some headed for the shoot-out scene, while others rushed down the street in a hurry to get themselves lost and forgotten before the law arrived.

Tamura emerged from the street-level door of the building across the street, gesturing toward a trio of special-squad operatives who were rounding the corner. He'd kept them in reserve in case the assassination attempt hadn't gone the way he and Bolan had planned.

As the special squad took control of the crowd, Tamura ushered Bolan to an unmarked security car parked near the corner.

As they drove off through the neon-tainted night, the security chief nodded at the big man with respect. He'd known Bolan was skilled. The battle at the Hakone hardsite had proved that. But until now he hadn't seen those skills in action. The closely choreographed combat made him think that perhaps Bolan could fight his way through the champions to Kuro after all.

Obviously the man had earned his scars. And the trust that Hal Brognola placed in him.

"The battle was ours all the way," Tamura remarked. "A clear victory. You match the claims made for you."

"We did it together," Bolan replied. "Thanks for covering me the way you did." He sat back in the seat and forced himself to relax, purging the tension that had wired his body ever since he'd left Club Scandinavia. He replayed every step of the ambush in his mind, figuring if there was a better way they could have done it. No, not really, he thought as they passed Shinjuku Station. It went down the way it could have.

"Too bad we didn't get any leads," Bolan said. "If we'd kept one of them alive—"

"We might be dead. It's victory enough that you're still alive. The clan will be wary now. Taro Kuro has given up too many of their ghosts. They'll think twice before coming after you again. And that fear will be one of our greatest allies. Perhaps some of them will even come over to our side."

Bolan nodded, but he didn't put too much faith in Tamura's statement. They both knew that defectors from the cult were rare indeed.

The Unseen Powers wouldn't stop until their last champion fell. If that's what it took, the Executioner would have to face them all, man, ghost or god.

7

The Japanese Intelligence officer glided across the stone terrace of Kannon Temple, the five-story pagoda complex in Asakusa Park.

He looked agitated today, Bolan thought, watching Tamura's approach from a bench along the concourse.

Late-afternoon crowds strolled through the temple grounds and shops in the huge park that sprawled through the heart of old Tokyo. The spring sun shone brightly on the vendor stalls and circular kiosks leading to the temple gates, basking the area in warmth. Perhaps it was a bit too warm for Mako Tamura, Bolan thought, noticing the beads of sweat on his forehead.

He no longer seemed the calm professional spook. Today he looked like one more harried businessman carrying a corporate cross on his shoulders.

Bolan draped his right arm over the back of the bench, stretching his long legs out in front of him as he gestured with his other hand for Tamura to join him. The quickest way to find out what was wrong with the Japanese was to stay calm enough for the two of them.

Tamura came to a sudden stop in front of the bench, his shadow blocking out the sun. "Were you working last night?" he asked, his voice cold and businesslike.

Bolan shrugged. "Why?" he asked. "We got some kind of situation here?"

"That depends." He dropped down on the bench next to Bolan.

"Uh-huh." Bolan noticed a quartet of blue-suited men in black glasses stop about forty yards away, two of them taking a sudden interest in religious artifacts at a vendor's stall. Though they handled several ivory figures and pretended to study them, they were obviously more interested in Bolan.

"Are they here to slap my wrists?" Bolan asked, gesturing toward the security men. "Or slap some cuffs on me? What's the deal?"

"That's what I have to find out."

"So start finding."

"All right," Tamura said. "Answer my question. Were you working last night?"

"That depends."

"On what?"

"On what you call working," Bolan replied. "I'm sure as hell not here on vacation. Otherwise I'd be standing in line on the slopes of Mount Fuji with a loaded camera."

"So?"

"So take it for granted I was busy."

"Where?" The Japanese Intelligence man managed to keep his voice cool, but his eyes betrayed his urgency.

"I had some meetings."

"I see. And did everyone walk away from these meetings?"

Bolan got his gist. "Yeah. It was a relatively peaceful sitdown with Hal and a couple of other white hats. No stretchers required."

Tamura nodded. "All right, then," he said, looking relieved. It was something he could check out easily enough.

"Why all the Peter Lorre business?" Bolan asked.

"What?"

"All of a sudden you were turning sinister on me. I thought we'd gone past the secret-handshake-and-decoder-ring stage. We know each other, guy. We've been through it together. What happened to change your mind?"

Tamura told him.

The previous night, just two days after the failed assassination attempt, the Unseen Powers did some housecleaning at Club Scandinavia. Two lower-level clan members who hung around the club were found dead in a wrecked car about ten miles outside the city on the road to Hakone.

"Accidents happen," Bolan commented.

"Yes," Tamura replied. "These men accidentally walked in front of a stream of bullets. They were dead long before their car went up in flames."

"And you thought I had something to do with it."

"Yes."

"Look," Bolan said, "you and I worked out a game plan. As far as I know, nothing's changed. You help point me in the right direction, and that's where I go. Before I go off on my own, I'll let you know."

"Thank you."

"What's bothering you about the two clansmen who got taken out?" Bolan asked. "Looks like a cause for celebration to me. Unless, of course, you were running them."

"No." Tamura mopped the sweat from his brow with the back of his hand. "Not those two."

"Who, then?"

"There was a snitch of mine—no, make that a friend of mine—who also worked at the club." The security man's soft voice was edged with bitterness.

That was why he'd come on so strong in the beginning, the Executioner realized. Obviously the death toll hadn't stopped at two. The clan had managed to hurt someone else, someone close to Tamura, and it had occurred to the man that Bolan might have played cowboy after all, going after the clan with six-guns blazing. And in retaliation the clan went after Tamura's friend.

"I don't take chances with innocent people's lives," Bolan told him. "Hell, they're the ones we're fighting for."

"I know that now." The man sighed and looked down at his feet. "The truth is, I knew that even before I called your hotel to set up the rendezvous. But I had to ask anyway. It's got me unsettled."

"Who else did they hit?" Bolan asked. "The Dagmar girl?"

Tamura gave him a questioning look.

"The blonde at the club. The dancer. Since you didn't give me her name, I gave her one myself. Did they hurt her?"

"No, she's fine...for the moment." Clouds of sorrow shaded his eyes as he continued. "It was a friend of mine from the old days who got burned. Someone who wanted the sect to get back to its real roots and turn away from the bandit clan it's become."

"He kept you informed?"

"Yes, and in turn I kept him out of jail on the minor crimes he committed to maintain his cover. He tried to help me. For that he died horribly."

"How did it happen?"

Tamura took a deep breath. "This morning I received a call at my headquarters. A person speaking with a muffled voice said that someone wanted to talk to me downstairs, then hung up. At that same moment a courier delivered a package for me. It was a hatbox, and inside was a severed head.''

"Your friend."

He nodded. ''The cut that killed him was clean. A sword strike. But it was the last of many. His face had been—'' The images flooded him then, and it took a moment for the man to regain his composure. ''A note was nailed to his tongue. It said he and I could talk again—when I catch up with him.''

Bolan felt a primitive urge well up inside him. It was the urge to strike out in vengeance at the clan. Unless men like he and Tamura crushed the serpents beneath their heels, the poison would spread.

But justice had to wait. For now. They had to dismember the clan bit by bit and earn their shot at the top. Otherwise too many innocent people would die. That was the advantage the clan had. They had limitless targets to strike out at.

He listened carefully as Tamura outlined what was going on with the clan. The first two deaths had been a ritual purging. Obviously Kuro hadn't been sure who had betrayed the clan's assassination plot, but he had to look omniscient to the rest of the clan. And so he killed two men who were merely under suspicion along with the one man he knew for certain was working with the Security Bureau.

"No doubt there will be more deaths," Tamura said. "These things have a way of getting out of hand.

We'll play it up in the media to give the clan a black eye in public—and set the stage for our next moves.''

"What about the rest of your ears in the clan? Can we count on any more information from them?''

Mako paused for a moment, as if he were thinking of withholding the information. But the suspicion that brought him to call the meeting in the first place was gone now. "We're in the process of pulling out the blonde, the only snitch left in the club. But we're doing it slowly so that it looks natural. If we haul her out of there too fast, it'll be like placing a bounty on her head. The clan will suspect her and hunt her down. Until we get her, our people will be all over the place. She'll be safe.''

"Any others?''

"A couple. One of them you'll meet—if you get that far. He's right on the island with Kuro.''

"A deadly place to be," Bolan observed.

"Yes, but he's quite deadly himself. That's another reason I wanted us to meet,'' he went on. "We've picked up word that the clan is going to make an attempt on JEICO again. You've damaged them where it hurts, and they've lost face. Before they send another champion against you, they'll try to show their people they can still win.''

"We're on the same wavelength," Bolan said. "That's what my meeting with Hal was about. Justice has picked up some disturbing Intelligence on some

JEICO operations. It looks like the clan's getting ready to do battle in the boardroom."

"This is what we didn't want to happen," Tamura replied. "The clan's tenuous code of honor has been stretched to the breaking point. They'll do whatever they have to to come out on top."

Bolan gripped the slats of the bench, slowly pushing himself upright. "I'll be waiting for them."

The security chief looked surprised.

"They activated my cover as a consultant with JEICO."

"Really? What's the position?"

"Headhunter," Bolan replied.

"Good hunting."

THE PARADE OF LIMOUSINES wound through the streets of Tokyo, carrying their kings of commerce. A summit meeting of JEICO executives had been called, attracting the top corporate honchos from both the American and Japanese sides.

One by one the rented limos and company cars dropped off their cargo at the entrance of the modern hotel in the middle of the Chiyoda-ku district. Like a small upscale city, the towering hotel complex boasted luxuries to rival the Imperial Palace, which guests could view from the upper floors.

Rooftop gardens and cafés, several top-rated restaurants, fashion shops and boutiques catered to the wealthy guests all under one roof. Despite the huge size of the hotel, it was able to maintain a strong sense of community. The staff had been trained to make everyone feel at home.

Like global geisha girls, the hotel boasted a large contingent of attractive well-educated women who were fluent in several languages and could help guests conduct their business anywhere in the world.

It was a hybrid of Western glitz and Eastern atmosphere, a perfect haunt for the JEICO chiefs.

And for Mack Bolan.

He was attending the three-day conference in the guise of an American engineering consultant. His disguise was simple. Temporary silver-colored spray aged him about twenty years, thick-framed glasses with nonprescription lenses gave him a professional look and his conservative blue suit was tailored to make him look a bit bulkier than his normal lean frame. At the same time the suit provided ample room for the concealment of the shoulder holster that held his Beretta.

Operating under the Rance Pollock persona, the cover identity that Hal Brognola had prepared for him well in advance, Bolan had already handed out several business cards that identified him as a consulting engineer for a subsidiary of one of the U.S. corporations working for JEICO.

The business cards were a vital part of Japanese culture. Considered as badges of respect, they indicated your position and how you were to be treated or addressed. The Rance Pollock card was very thorough. It had American lettering on one side and a Japanese translation on the other.

Bolan had accepted several cards from Japanese general managers and division chiefs whom he'd been introduced to for the first time tonight—although he knew most of them from their dossiers.

The cards were just one part of creating a working identity. Brognola had also booked a room for him at the hotel. In that room, just before the evening kicked off, Brognola gave him a refresher course on the various defense projects JEICO was working on so that Bolan could hold his own in conversation with the executives.

Although there were several other complementary projects in the works, the ones that Hal Brognola was overseeing for the government were the rail gun projects and the space plane prototypes. The electromagnetic rail guns could hurl armor-piercing projectiles at speeds up to twenty-five miles per second. Intended to intercept ballistic missiles, the rail guns were being designed for ground-based systems and spaced-based weapons platforms. Like computers in their infancy, the current designs were workable but massive. The emphasis was on miniaturization, a field in which the Japanese excelled.

The other program attracting a lot of development dollars was the space plane or transatmospheric vehicle. It was a manned aircraft that could take off from a conventional runway, go into orbit for recon, satellite repair, or combat missions and touch down on a runway.

It was the wave of the future and would either take over from the space shuttle or at least reduce the need for so many dollar-draining shuttle launches.

Bolan knew the reasons behind the joint project. Like it or not, the U.S. and Japan were linked in the development and application of high technology. If they went their separate ways across the board, the resulting economic warfare could be devastating for both nations. This way they would share in costs and profits. Meanwhile, each country still was developing their own projects in other areas.

The technical aspects were familiar enough to Bolan. He didn't want a doctorate in space-based weaponry. He just wanted to know enough to pass himself off as an insider while he scouted for others who didn't belong—like members of the Unseen Powers.

Another thing that bolstered Bolan's disguise was the confident attitude he projected—that he was one of them, that he belonged there. And though it was his least favorite place to be, surrounded by people from the business world, the warrior put on an appropriate mask and carried around a drink that he seldom touched.

It was the first night of the summit meeting, the icebreaker. There was dinner, drinks and dancing in a ballroom on the western wing of the hotel. It was a subdued but elegant atmosphere, with moonlight basking the dance floor through a slanted glass roof, giving the guests the feeling they were in an observatory.

Bolan did a lot of watching, observing some of the executives who were suspected of collaboration with the Unseen Powers.

Midway through the evening, while an orchestra of tuxedoed Japanese musicians played American standards, Hal Brognola drifted over his way, escorting a woman who looked to be half his age.

"This is Caroline Langone," Brognola said. "She's been working security for the JEICO operation."

The Executioner looked down at her, finding himself entranced. Red haired, she was wrapped in a clinging red dress with a neckline that revealed a generous amount of cleavage. She sported dangling earrings that glittered like hidden treasure beneath her hair. She looked like part of the entertainment, a torch singer rather than a security specialist.

"The eyes and ears of Uncle Sam never looked so lovely," Bolan said sincerely.

"Thanks for the compliment. Allow me to do the same."

"Shoot."

"I'll leave that to you," she replied, dropping her eyes for a split second. "As for *your* compliment, let's just say that I've never seen anyone age so gracefully—or so quickly."

Bolan exchanged looks with Brognola. Obviously she'd been brought into the know, a professional courtesy he wouldn't complain about. There was no sense in taking the risk of being blown away by your own Intelligence people.

Her presence with Brognola meant that she was high up in security circles and could wield a lot of power. Definitely a woman to watch—and to watch out for. He'd been told there was a high-ranking woman operative on the scene. He just hadn't been told how much of an operator she was.

"You seem to know a lot about me," he commented.

"Not nearly enough," she replied, the soft scent of violets wafting in front of her as she stepped in close to him. "After all, we're supposed to be old friends."

Bolan nodded. "I'm sure we have many fond memories together."

Her red-hued lips pursed into a smile as she reached up and fingered his tie.

"It doesn't need straightening."

"Oh? What does?"

The warrior smiled and dropped his hand to the small of her back, resting it on the soft curve of her hips as he led her to the dance floor.

He guided her through the throng of gray-haired corporate chieftains, many of them dancing with women even younger than Caroline, women who cast looks at her as though she were the enemy.

With the star-specked night gleaming through the glass roof, Bolan felt like an alien for a moment, cut off from the world the rest of the people in the room lived in, a world of work and play and small victories.

He'd made his choice long ago, or rather, his choice had been made for him. Fate had made him a soldier, and Fate had kept him on active duty ever since.

The music stopped.

Bolan edged the woman from the dance floor to an alcove where a sliver of glass looked out on Imperial Park. Though it looked as if the two of them were chatting and flirting in a cozy spot of their own, they were going over security matters.

"How much do you really know about JEICO, the cult and the killings?" Bolan asked.

"Whatever people don't want me to know, that's what I know," she said.

"And how do you find all that out?"

"Any way I can." She laughed, a soft intimate sound that would disarm any man. "That's part of my job description."

"I'm sure you do a good job."

"Everyone seems to think so," she agreed.

"No argument there." Though Langone didn't look like a security pro, it made a lot of sense to have her aboard in that capacity. Most Japanese businessmen connected to JEICO weren't used to dealing with women in the corporate sector. Instead of taking her seriously as an executive, they'd consider her an ornamentation, a bright plaything for her superior. It would take an even greater leap of the imagination to suspect her of being security.

That meant she could do a lot of serious investigating.

So far she'd uncovered the most likely target for the Unseen Powers. For several days running he'd been shadowed by unidentified men, who in turn were watched closely by the Security Bureau and Langone's own surveillance teams.

His name was Saburo Watanabe, an owllike man with a pleasant but alert gaze. He was round-shouldered and kept his arms tucked close to his sides, nodding his head now and then when one of his subordinates looked to him for direction.

Though Watanabe hardly spoke, his subordinates seldom said anything without his approval. As Bolan watched the small group gathered around the man, it reminded him of a stage play. Watanabe was the director, and his blue-suited subordinates were his well-rehearsed actors.

He was also the director of many crucial JEICO operations. One of the project's top minds, his knowledge was needed in several different disciplines. That made him a potential gold mine for the Unseen Powers. And, Bolan thought, if things were handled right, a land mine. They might make the wrong step.

Both U.S. and Japanese Intelligence believed another kidnap attempt was going to be made and that Watanabe was the most likely candidate. Instead of stealing sensitive information, the sect would steal the man who held it. Not only could they pick his brain for information, but they could also hold him for ransom.

"Things could get rough around here," Bolan commented.

"I can handle myself," she said.

"I'm sure you can. But there's a chance you'll have to shed your disguise."

"Only if you promise to help."

He arched an eyebrow. "That's an easy enough promise to keep. If the time's right—and you're still around."

"What do you mean?"

"Once your cover's blown, you'll be fair game for the clan."

"I've got people covering me," she said.

"Yeah, I'm sure you do. But I don't think you know how these people work. The clan takes everything personally. Kill one, you'll have to kill them all. They'll come back at you one by one, each assassin better than the last."

Her face grew pale. "Why are you telling me all this?" she asked, a hint of anger in her voice.

"I don't want to spoil your party," he said. "I just want you to be ready when the time comes."

"I *am* ready. Wait'll you see me in action."

"I already have," he replied. "And I like what I see."

8

A woman in a black dress drifted through the entrance of the Chiyoda-ku hotel, escorted by a tall and slender man whose smile was as warm as bared fangs.

It was the second night of the JEICO conference, and it was the first night Yukiko was in command.

"Be yourself," the woman hissed.

"If I was being myself, I wouldn't be here," the man replied grimly.

It was true, she thought. Jiro was here under protest. Like many clansmen, he'd grown tired of the series of defeats handed to the Unseen Powers. For a man used to working in the dark, walking into a brightly lit fortress of wealth seemed as inviting as laying his head on a chopping block.

But he had no say in the matter.

"Just drop the smile," Yukiko warned. "On you it looks like a death mask."

"Yes, *sir*," he said, making it clear he didn't like being accountable to a woman. But he liked living, so he followed her command. He dropped the smile and assumed a nonchalant air as he squired her past the hotel desk.

Jiro was a gaunt-faced man with a sallow cadaverous complexion. It was deceiving, making him look broom thin and sickly. But he was one of the clan's most capable assassins. His pallor was due to his vampiric habits. Like a nocturnal creature of prey he did his best work at night.

Several more members of the Unseen Powers filtered into the hotel like ghostly gate-crashers, none of them standing out from the rest of the guests. They looked like typical Japanese businessmen in their corporate blues, but carried businesslike weapons in their briefcases.

Yukiko had also dressed for the occasion. She looked like a picture-perfect corporate wife. Her black dress was snug on the hips, with inverted notches revealing a glimpse of stockinged thigh. It was mildly adventurous, but nothing that would stand out from what the other corporate wives would be wearing at the gathering.

Pretending not to know one another, the clansmen drifted through the lobby, the bars, the shops, then made their way one by one to the block of rooms on the third floor.

Just opposite the elevator banks, the rooms had been booked in advance by go-betweens for the clan, serving as the forward operating base for the hotel commandos. JEICO's gathering was being held in a nightclub on the fourth floor, making it perfect for a hit and git. If it was any higher, the clansmen would run the risk of being cut off in the honeycomb of rooms and have to fight their way out.

This way they could do it right—hit fast and usher their quarry out. If anything went wrong, escape was only a few flights down.

Sitting in one of the middle rooms in front of a black-lacquered vanity, Yukiko struck a match to her filterless cigarette and blew the harsh smoke at the curved mirror. It billowed like a fog on the reflecting glass and gave her a ghostly visage. Like an oracle on the mountain, she stared at her image and tried to divine the outcome of tonight's attempt.

A strange light sparkled in her eyes, as though some higher intelligence were looking back at her.

The eyes looked back with approval.

It would work. After all, she was only heeding the celestial voices and visions that had come to her these past few nights. Yukiko herself had received guidance from the Unseen Powers this time, her familiar spirits taking the place of Kuro's visions.

Lately Kuro's visions had been weak, sometimes totally misleading. That was a secret the two of them kept to themselves, although she enjoyed it in a perverse way. As long as Kuro was out of favor with the gods, her own powers could emerge.

"When do we do it?" Jiro asked, pacing beside her. He was frowning, whether at seeing Yukiko smoke or simply because she was the one who gave the orders—it was hard to tell. He was on edge.

She looked at her watch. "Soon. The others will be here soon."

Jiro nodded. The two other men in the room gave him a wide berth as he paced back and forth like a gladiator about to step into the arena.

THE JAPANESE MAN could pass as a secret-service agent in any country. Tinted glasses hid his eyes, his hair was cut short in a military style and he wore a suit so immaculately pressed it looked like a uniform.

But despite his military bearing and the impressive credentials in his wallet, Iwai Kobayushi wasn't working undercover for the Japanese government.

He was working undercover for the Unseen Powers.

So was Naoto, the man walking next to him in the carefully rehearsed role of a subordinate.

Carrying slim black leather attaché cases, both men walked into the hotel as if they were ready to take charge of slipshod security.

Which is exactly what they did.

At the check-in desk Kobayushi demanded to see the hotel's head of security. A young guard immediately showed them to a back room on the first floor. There, behind a desk awash in a sea of paperwork and swivel monitors, sat a worried man in wire-rimmed spectacles who looked more like a clerk than head of security.

The man stood to receive the "government officials," at the same time dismissing the younger guard.

"No," Kobayushi said. "It's better if he stays. He should hear what we have to say." He nodded to the security guard, who took one of the chairs that flanked the desk.

Naoto closed the door.

With a crisp gesture Kobayushi unfolded his wallet to display his fake credentials. Then, while the hotel man studied them, he took him into his confidence immediately—overwhelming the man's normal caution with a sense of urgency. "We have just received word there'll be an attack on the JEICO party tonight."

The manager recoiled but did his best to hide his shock. "I see," he said. "But, as arranged, details of security have been left with the JEICO officials. They're in charge—"

"Exactly the problem," Kobayushi replied. "It will be an inside job. Either Japanese or American security officials are in on the plot."

The hotel man still looked stunned, but there was also a hint of joy on his narrow face. He was obviously pleased to be involved in such delicate matters, taken into the confidence of such a high-ranking member of the Security Bureau.

"Quickly," Kobayushi said to the man. "Explain hotel security procedures, methods of gaining access to the JEICO rooms and the number of armed guards employed by the hotel."

The man nodded. Feeling as if he'd just been drafted into espionage service, he ran down the usual methods of hotel security. Then, at Kobayushi's urging, he showed him the computer-coded pass cards that got entry anywhere in the hotel.

"Very professional," the U.P Clansman praised. "You've helped us a good deal. Now, there's one more thing. The armed guard you said patrols the first floor—obviously a good man. Very discreet, whoever he is. We didn't even see him, but we don't want him to be hurt. Nor do we want him to hurt other members of our team. He must be told what's going on. Please call him in."

Three minutes later an average-looking man in a casual jacket knocked. Naoto opened the door slightly, just enough for the man to stick his head into the room.

"You called," the new arrival said. "Is there a problem?"

"Please come in," the security man replied. "There are some things these men have to tell you."

While the armed guard stepped into the room, Kobayushi set his attaché case on the edge of the desk, flicking open the hasps.

The moment Naoto closed the door behind the guard, Kobayushi spun around.

The guard's eyes had grown wary, and now they turned vacant as the U.P. fighter drilled him in the forehead with a round from a silenced stainless-steel Navy Colt .22.

Continuing his spin, Kobayushi bore down on the security head and triggered another round, exploding a gout of blood from the man's chest. His mouth opened, gasping loudly until, almost as an afterthought, Kobayushi shot him again—this time in the head.

The remaining security guard, who'd been staring at the gunman as if he belonged in someone else's nightmare, finally reacted. He was halfway out of his chair when Naoto sprang forward and dealt the man a crushing blow to his trachea.

As the guard bounced against the wall and fell, his assailant dropped a hammerfist to the back of his skull. The sickening crack was followed by a soft thump as the man's forehead smashed onto the desk. He slumped onto the floor, his arms spreading out as if in supplication.

Kobayushi replaced the murder weapon into the briefcase while Naoto took the coded computer cards from the security men. Then the two clansmen left the room, locking the door securely behind them before making their way to the elevator.

They ascended to the third floor, got off and walked through the wide-open door of the room across from the elevator.

Kobayushi stepped to the center of the room and held his attaché case calmly in front of him. He wore a thin smile on his face, like a man who'd just closed an important deal.

"How did it go?" Yukiko asked.

"The only way it could."

"Did they give you any trouble?"

"Just like the hotel advertises," the man replied, "'Nothing too much to ask for.' They were quite helpful before we sent them on their way."

Yukiko barely registered the news of the deaths. It was just another detail to her, a few more obstacles cleared out of the way. "You've got the cards?"

Kobayushi nodded and gestured toward Naoto, who removed a trio of computer-coded pass cards from his pocket. "Tickets to anywhere in the hotel," he announced.

"Beautiful." Yukiko was unable to hide the excitement in her voice. "Now let's get ready to join the party. We don't want to keep Mr. Watanabe waiting."

The clansmen took out their heavy-metal invitations and slapped in fresh magazines.

ICE WATER IN HIS HAND and ice in his eyes, the Executioner scanned the packed room. He idly swirled the glass in his hands, clinking the ice cubes together. Then he took another sip, adding to his cover as just another gray-haired executive who had had too much to drink tonight. And judging from the deliberately bulky suit he wore, perhaps too much to eat.

So far the second night of JEICO festivities had been a success. Not just from the social end. Tonight's gathering was held in a smaller, more private nightclub on the fourth floor of the hotel.

Several alcoves pinwheeled like plush spokes from a shale-stone oasis in the center of the room where dwarf trees surrounded a softly gurgling fountain. A flight of stairs led up toward each alcove, where separate JEICO cliques toasted and roasted one another.

Good cover, Bolan thought, standing near the sunken fountain. From his vantage point he could see every section of the room and get there in a hurry if he had to.

His eyes kept returning to Watanabe. As usual, the owllike executive was surrounded by several younger corporate types. Though many of their faces were different from the previous night's gathering, nothing looked out of place.

"Welcome aboard, Pollock."

Bolan turned toward a heavyset man who needed little effort to portray a drunk. The man's eyes were glazed. He was either having religious visions or he was half-cut. His outstretched hand barely preceded his girth.

As Bolan shook his hand, the man said, "Name's Carson. Friends call me Kit."

Since there were precious few friends in sight, the man had zeroed in on Bolan.

"Rance Pollock." Bolan had seen Carson the previous night and had carefully avoided him, having seen his dossier well in advance.

"Right," Carson replied. "Know all about you."

The man's voice was loud. Too loud. Bolan stepped a few feet away, nodding his head for Carson to follow. Then, his hard eyes boring into him, the Executioner said, "What is it you think you know about me?"

"Everything. Hell, that's my job, after all. Don't tell anybody—" he leaned forward in a conspiratorial gesture "—but I think we're working for the same... Company."

"I don't have to tell anyone," the warrior said stonily. "You're doing a fine job yourself." The man had done everything but wear a badge saying Made In Langley.

Carson should have been sent on a permanent vacation years ago, Bolan thought, or parked behind a Company desk somewhere out of the line of fire. Whoever had posted him to this hot site was playing with dynamite.

The Executioner knew his type well. The man used to do good work for the CIA, and somewhere along the way he'd been hurt bad. Instead of his body, it was his mind that was shot. Too many years on the covert trenches had turned him into an alcoholic.

But his real problem was that he didn't know he had a problem, and his control officer hadn't seen fit to tell him otherwise. Carson thought he was still one of the Company cowboys, or as some of the spooks called his type, a "Double-G," which stood for guerrilla-gorilla. Long on strength, short on wit. You pointed them in the right direction and let them loose on the enemy.

His fighting days were over, but somehow on the way to pasture, the Company attached him to the JEICO operation. It wasn't for old times' sake, either. The man was a living, breathing decoy. Nothing else. A sacrificial lamb. There was no way he'd be able to keep his part of the security detail secret, so the Company had used him to leak selected details about JEICO operations to Unseen Powers.

Now through his gin fog, Carson was talking about Bolan's cover identity.

"I'm an engineering consultant. Pure and simple."

"Yeah," Carson said, "that's what all the background on you says. But, hey, I know how to fill in the blanks, you know."

Since exchanging tradecraft with a drunk wasn't the best way of maintaining his cover, Bolan decided to seek out Caroline Langone and tell her to keep a tighter leash on the man. After all, she was one of the security crew responsible for keeping him on.

"Look, guy," Bolan said, "I'm a troubleshooter. Let's leave it at that."

"Now that's something I'll buy. You and me, we don't fit in with all these suits."

"You and me better keep our aces up our sleeves," Bolan told him. "No sense in letting the opposition see us together. Right?"

"You got it."

Bolan drifted up one of the staircases and caught Langone's eye. She broke away from a group of executives who were soliciting her opinion on JEICO affairs.

"What is it?" she asked.

"Carson."

"Oh. Right."

"He's a weak link in the operation," Bolan said. "He shouldn't be here."

"I agree. But Carson doesn't. He thinks he's a vital part of the operation—"

"When in fact he's just a little fish you tossed out on the waters to watch the sharks that come after him."

"Look," Langone stated, "the Company is all he has left. If he wants to stay in the game, then he has to play the hand he's dealt."

"You're a real softy."

She shrugged and looked at the Executioner matter-of-factly. "There are no saints here. Not one of us. Now, if you'll excuse me, I've got Company business to attend to." She looked over at Watanabe, another sacrificial lamb—although the man had known the stakes from the git-go.

THE NIGHTCLUB on the fourth floor had three entrances. Yukiko and Jiro walked down the corridor toward the main one, a pair of oval glass doors that faced a small waiting area of red leather couches and low tables. The area was deserted except for Iwai Kobayushi, who'd preceded them just a couple of minutes earlier. He sat on one of the couches reading the evening edition of a newspaper.

The man looked totally relaxed, as though he were waiting for one of his superiors inside the club. He didn't look up as his confederates passed.

Yukiko laughed softly, as if the gaunt giant had just said something amusing. Only she could see Jiro's eyes, however, and it was not laughter that lurked within.

Once they stepped past the glass doors, a security man in evening dress discreetly looked on while the doormen inspected their invitation. It was a legitimate one, complete with a "hidden" identification mark that one of the clansmen who'd infiltrated JEICO had obtained for them.

As soon as Yukiko and her accomplice gained entrance, Kobayushi stood and lit a cigarette. He walked around the corner and glanced toward the stairway at the end of the corridor. Through a square, meshed glass window in the door, he saw Naoto watching him.

He took a long puff on the cigarette, then nodded.

The clansmen streamed through the door, heading for the service-and-employee entrance to their left, wielding the pass cards that would let them in.

Then Kobayushi headed back to the main entrance.

The fireworks were about to begin.

BOLAN WATCHED the petite black-haired siren drift toward the bar with her escort. There was something about her that seemed familiar...her figure, her walk. She moved like an athlete in competition—Yukiko! Her hair was longer, extravagantly curled, but that was her beneath the wig.

In a nonchalant gesture Bolan raised his glass as if he were greeting a friend at the opposite side of the room.

The friend was Mako Tamura. The Security Bureau man glided across the floor and met the Executioner halfway.

"What is it?"

Bolan nodded toward Yukiko and her escort, who were nonchalantly heading toward Watanabe's group, drinks in hand. "The goddess is here."

"Yes. And that means so are her worshipers."

In a series of imperceptible signals, Tamura alerted his security team.

NAOTO BURST through the service doors into the kitchen, heading up a team of clansmen. He shouted a stream of orders in a voice that paralyzed the kitchen staff.

At first the cooks and waiters stared at the well-dressed men, not understanding what was going on. But then they registered the fact that the business end of several automatic weapons were pointed in their direction. They dropped to the floor before Naoto had to say another word.

The clansmen charged through the kitchen, stepping over the prone workers as if they were human debris, then they burst into the nightclub.

At the same time a single file of clansmen raced from the employees' quarters, waving a deadly assortment of silenced submachine guns and machine pistols.

They looked for Yukiko and saw her pinpointing their target—a very startled Watanabe, who was backing away from the men around him.

Naoto fired a warning burst into the ceiling, shattering a bank of overhead lights that popped, then fell to the floor in a rain of shards.

Then the real shooting started.

But it wasn't from the clansmen.

The men ringing Watanabe were Security Bureau sharpshooters who had stepped in front of him the moment the killers burst into the room. They unholstered their automatics and triggered a full-auto barrage into the charging gunmen.

The carnage was devastating. One moment the clansmen were primed to wreak havoc; the next they were tasting their own blood as the lead fusillade stormed through their ranks.

Naoto fell in the first volley, two other clansmen dropping on top of his prostrate form, their vacant eyes staring toward the ceiling.

The target was no longer in sight.

As soon as the shooting had started, Watanabe was hustled out of sight. As arranged, he was shielded by the huge table put into position earlier that night—and by the human shield formed by the antiterrorist squad.

They formed a half circle in front of Watanabe's cover, standing their ground while the clan shock troops tried to regroup and launch another attack.

BOLAN STEPPED toward the rock wall on the edge of the sunken fountain area, his Beretta effectively catching the clansmen in a cross fire. With staggered bursts he opened up holes in the ranks of the single file of armed men.

One of the phony businessmen turned and leveled his subgun, the weapon spitting fire and carving into the floor a wood-splintering trail that chewed its way toward the Executioner.

But the trail came to an abrupt halt when Bolan chopped a trio of 9 mm slugs through his gut. The gunner folded over and crumpled to the floor.

Alerted by a flash of movement to his right, the warrior turned and spotted another clansman rushing for him. This time the man's weapon was already trained on the Executioner. Fighting the urge to keep moving and dive for cover, Bolan's combat sense took over. He dropped flat on his back, coming down hard on the stone, while a burst of autofire sliced through the air to his right, where the gunman had expected him to move.

The impact of the fall knocked the wind from Bolan. Overriding the choking sensation that squeezed his chest, the warrior kicked his feet against the stone floor, digging in his heels for all he was worth. He propelled himself closer to the wall and got out of the man's field of fire.

Just then the clansman sprinted to the edge of the rock wall, splitting the air with a war cry as he hurried to finish off his prey.

Flat on his back with the Beretta nosing upward, the Executioner squeezed off one round as soon as the man was above him. Like a 9 mm metal bit, the slug drilled a hole in the man's chin, traveled straight up through his skull and held him tottering in suspended animation for a few moments before he toppled headfirst onto the stone.

Bolan got to his feet and slapped another magazine into the Beretta, surveying the killing ground.

Angry shouts from the clansmen mixed in with the chorus of screams from the JEICO civilians as a contagion of panic spread through the room. Pandemonium reigned.

The Executioner stepped into the fray.

CAROLINE LANGONE FROZE the moment the action started. Not out of fear, but out of concern for the setup. She looked around the room to make sure the jaws of the trap were ready to spring shut. The woman had been instrumental in designing the ruse with Mako Tamura, replacing Watanabe's corporate coterie with armed men. She'd also positioned other Company operatives throughout the crowd to pose as JEICO officials.

Everyone had followed their instructions perfectly, she thought.

Almost everyone.

She saw Carson staggering around in the midst of the chaos, looking as if he were lost in traffic. His eyes flicked from one spot to another, trying to find the right way out of the mess. Somehow in his drunkard's walk, the aging CIA warhorse had managed to stumble into the last pocket of resistance.

Yukiko had fled the moment the attack blew up in her face, hurrying toward the main entrance, where two other clansmen covered her retreat.

But her deadly escort remained. Jiro took control of the clan's fighters and shouted out orders as he went into action.

He flew across the room in a last-ditch effort to salvage the kidnapping attempt. His long legs moved with an unexpected grace as he leapt over a fallen security man, touched down briefly on the floor, then spun around, his left foot flying in a reverse hook kick.

The flat of his foot caught one of Tamura's officers in the jaw, breaking the bone and launching the man into the air in an explosion of blood. Jiro grabbed the man's weapon and fired a burst that punched another officer off his feet.

Bolan caught the action from the corner of his eye as he and Tamura closed in on two clansmen trying to grab hostages. One clansman waved a blade with his right hand as his left curled around the waist of a frightened blond-haired debutante.

Like a magnet drawn to steel, Tamura tackled the clansman, who released his prize under the ferocity of the attack. The security chief pulled back on the man's wrist until there was a crack.

The other potential hostage was a silver-haired executive who tumbled over like a scarecrow when the clansman grabbed for him. He managed to topple over one of the tables as he fell, breaking the clansman's grip.

Bolan landed on the gunman like a hammer, thumping his cocked elbow on his back, the force of the blow knocking the man facefirst onto the floor.

A blurring motion provided the warrior with a split second warning before he came under the attack of a clansman swinging a broken chair leg like a baseball bat. He lurched to his right and managed to keep his skull intact, but he caught the blow on his ribs and doubled over from the impact.

A snap kick intended for Bolan's face caught him on the breastbone and sent him reeling across the floor. He rolled onto his shoulders and slapped the carpet with his left hand to minimize the effects of the fall. With the Beretta rising in his steel grip, he triggered a burst at his attacker. The lanky clansman fell back, dead before he hit the floor.

JIRO SLICED through the security men, kicking and punching every step of the way. He was like a gaunt windmill, somehow all over the place at once but avoiding counterstrikes from the security team.

He broke through the last human barrier, then reached out to snare Watanabe. He grabbed the man's collar, twisted it and with a brutal yank lifted the round-shouldered executive to his feet.

As Jiro swung the barrel of his subgun toward Watanabe, he suddenly caught a ham fist on the back of his neck. Stunned by the blow, the clansman released his prey and turned to deal with his assailant.

It was Carson, who had lurched around the perimeter of the action, looking harmless, looking drunk. But his eyes were unclouded as he stared at the subgun homing in on him.

Jiro triggered a burst, but by then Carson had jumped forward. His hands clapped against the clansman's ears, exploding his eardrums.

Carson's body shuddered as he danced a dead man's two-step, but he didn't let go. He'd anchored himself on Jiro, clamping his hands around the back of his neck. And as he dropped to the floor like a stone, he broke Jiro's neck in the process.

The tall clansman pitched forward onto the floor.

Carson managed to make it halfway to his feet despite the bloody exit wounds that marked the point-blank burst he'd taken. More ghost than human, the CIA warhorse savored the stunned expressions on the security men who realized he was the one who saved Watanabe.

He opened his mouth and tried to talk, but the words wouldn't come. It didn't matter. Everyone who saw him knew what he was thinking. This was the way he wanted to go.

And then he went, collapsing on the floor with a loud thump.

It was over.

The silence was deafening.

The clansmen were silenced; the gunfire had stopped. A contingent of Tamura's security men bolted from the club in pursuit of Yukiko and the others who'd escaped.

Langone pushed through the crowd of civilians who got to their feet suddenly, as if they'd risen from the dead. She crouched amid the chaos and cradled Carson in her arms.

Bolan stepped through the trashed tables and chairs, and stood looking down at the slain operative.

He realized that Carson was good, that he hadn't been kept around only out of pity. A good part of his "drunk" image was an act. There was still enough of the guerrilla fighter inside of him to show itself when the time came.

Langone had suspected that all along, and he'd proved her right in the most final way.

She stood slowly and surveyed the damage. Everywhere she looked were signs of the battle—bullet holes stitched in the ceiling, bodies sprawled over tables, a dazed group of guests walking through the battlefield.

Bolan surveyed his own damage. He'd been hit hard in the hand-to-hand combat and now that it was over, his body was letting him know. But at least he came out of it standing up. The security unit had taken some heavy casualties.

Despite the chaos, it had gone as well as anyone could have hoped for. No one could be protected completely against the clan, but they had been more than ready when the attack had come, thanks to Langone's and Tamura's preparations.

As Bolan headed for the door, he looked over his shoulder at Caroline Langone. "Lady," he said, "you throw one hell of a party."

9

Wind scoured the island of Yamishima, howling in from the Pacific and shrieking around the fishing boats moored in the harbor. The shrieks always sounded worse at night. They spiraled down from the mountaintop and lashed at the single-story homes that were perched above the bay, rattling windows and souls alike.

The rough seas and the bitter breezes stirred that primitive part of man that suspected the earth was alive. And it was angry. On nights like this the men in the village believed that the island's unofficial name, Kamishima, was more appropriate. It was the isle of the gods, and the wind gave voice to their wrath.

It was a night meant for staying inside by the fire and the light, a night meant for admitting that the only real superpower in the world was nature.

It was also the night that a Japanese man in his sixties walked downhill from the slope upon which Taro Kuro's empire was built. He moved silently past the houses where Kuro's retainers lived, past the houses of the champions in waiting and waded deeper into the storm that raged around him.

His walking stick was carved from hardwood, and a finely detailed serpent wound around its full length. Gripping the dragon-jawed handle, the man moved downhill in the driving rain. The stick plunged into the mud now and then, and the slick earth tugged at his feet. But he never fell.

As the gusts kicked against the man's seemingly frail body, he moved in a steady gait that accepted the sodden slaps of wind. Regardless of what the night threw at him, he pressed unerringly forward.

It was much the same way he moved through life. No matter what was in his path, he found a way around it or through it.

His name was Haruki, but everyone called him "the sage."

Or they used to.

In the days when the Unseen Powers was a real sect, when men like Haruki were proud to be a part of the secret traditions, the warriors had come to him for counsel. These days few men listened to him anymore. Somehow Taro Kuro had wrested control from the gods themselves, stamping his own brand of heresy onto the religion that had been born on the island—like the sage himself.

A native shaman, he knew the rocky spine of the island as if it were his own body. And he was the soul, blackened and tattered by the deeds of Taro Kuro.

Over the years tracks of crow's-feet had etched their way across his weathered face, and his hair had turned the color of finely spun silver. But the sage's mind still struck like lightning. So did his hands and feet. He was a warrior, an adept. But in the beginning he, too, had been fooled by the emergence of Kuro, expecting great things of him. He'd looked for a god and instead found a demon.

Which was why Haruki was treading downhill in the middle of the storm—he had a rendezvous with one of Mako Tamura's men. Mako had left them long ago, but a part of his heart still beat on the island. He hadn't turned his back on the sect completely. Not yet. Not while men like the sage were still around.

Though Tamura's presence would be too notable on the island, an undercover operative could slip in and out easily enough. Since fishing boats constantly plied the coasts of Yamishima, it was a simple matter for a Security Bureau to drop a man onto the island and to make contact with the sage.

The security man had previously met with Haruki a number of times to determine if Kuro was residing on the island and to gauge the temperament of the clansmen.

Tonight was no exception.

His contact waited in the shadows of a series of stepping-stone ridges that dropped down to the sea. Haruki sensed him before he saw him, turning just as the man stepped forward, soaking wet and shrouded in a night-black raincoat.

"It is good of you to come on a night like this, Grandfather."

Haruki nodded. *Grandfather.* Few clansmen used the term with respect these days. To them it was a term of scorn used to dismiss him from war councils. But lately Kuro had even dismissed the clansmen from his council, listening instead to the sorceress, Yukiko.

"I haven't traveled nearly as far as you," Haruki replied. "Yours is the more dangerous path."

The men spoke hurriedly, aware that no night was forever safe from the eyes of the clan. Now and then Haruki looked back the way he'd come, listening intently for sounds that didn't belong.

The contact filled him in on some of the operations on the mainland, while Haruki told him of the temperament of the clan.

"Kuro is back from hiding?"

"Yes," Haruki said. "He returned earlier today—but now he's hiding from his own men."

The other man smiled. "There's trouble in the ranks?"

"A spark here and there. Not enough to ignite rebellion—but I toss kindling whenever I can. The clan is angered over the suicidal attack on the hotel. They feel Kuro spends their lives too freely. However, they're not yet ready to confront him. But if there's another defeat, then my counsel may sway them."

"What does Kuro plan to do?"

Haruki waved his hand in a fluttering motion. "It's easier to catch the wind than to learn his mind. Kuro walks a hundred paths at once and gets nowhere. But the goal remains the same—to keep the American at bay until the clan can triumph."

"That time may never come. I've seen the American in combat. We believe he's the same one his government calls the Executioner."

"The sacred Executioner," Haruki said. "Every faith must face such a creature. He must be a terrible man."

"No, not to you. But to men like Kuro he's a terror. The champions can't keep him away."

The two men talked a while longer before bringing the clandestine meeting to an end.

There'd be a few more meetings with Tamura's man, then the invisible empire would come crashing down. In the back of Haruki's mind lurked the hope that the sect could return to its roots and proudly wear its name once more.

But first they'd have to live through the night of the Executioner.

BOLAN FOLDED the carbine stock of the Beretta 93-R as he watched Haruki move safely into the uphill shadows. No clansman had shadowed the old man to the rendezvous. If he had, that man wouldn't have returned home tonight.

The warrior stepped carefully across the mud-slicked rocks, keeping a ready grip on the silenced 9 mm pistol. When he neared the ridge where the meeting had taken place, he scanned the area once again with the compact handheld thermal imager. The monocular night-vision device could see through mist and brush.

But tonight there'd been nothing to see except for the sage and Tamura's contact, a man Bolan knew only by his code name Haimyo. He was one of the special-guard commandos Tamura had seconded to the Security Bureau team for the duration of the operation against Kuro and the clan.

"Is the grandfather safe?" Haimyo asked when Bolan dropped down beside him on the slab of gray rock.

"Yeah, he's safe. The question is, can we trust him?"

"A good question." Haimyo adjusted the hood of his slicker. "So good that he asked the same about you."

"What did you tell him?"

"The truth. Otherwise he'd turn me into a lizard."

"If the man really is a shaman," Bolan said dryly, "why doesn't he just cast a spell on all of them?"

"He's working on it. In time he'll uncloud their eyes."

"Do you believe he really has powers?" Bolan asked curiously.

Haimyo shrugged. "I believe what I see. But I don't disbelieve him, either."

"That's my point. Don't get me wrong. If he casts a spell that stops bullets, I'll be the first in line. In the meantime, if we can convince the clan there's strong magic in the air..."

"You have something in mind?"

"Yeah," Bolan replied. "When D day comes, I've got an idea for some stage magic that might win some converts to our side—if I correctly understand the clan's beliefs. That's something you, I and Haruki can go over."

"You make it sound impossible."

"For an ordinary man, maybe, but for a shaman, nothing's impossible. I hope. From what I've seen, it's the only way to get past the champions up there." Bolan gestured toward the slope that led up to Kuro's sanctuary. The houses had been positioned well, forming a formidable gauntlet that he had to get past. "I'll have to put my faith in him."

"As good a faith as any. And the grandfather will have the same faith in you."

"How do you know that?" Bolan asked. "No one knows me here."

"Not by name, but by reputation. It has finally occurred to the clan that they're dealing with the man known as the Executioner."

Bolan grunted noncommittally and quickly guided the conversation back to Haruki. His cooperation was critical to the operation. Somehow they had to convince the rank and file of the clan to end the covert war of murder and extortion against JEICO. Otherwise, when Kuro fell, a new tyrant could take his place. Same demands, same war, same bloodshed. It was up to them to change the ways of the clan or bury it forever.

A gust of wind whipped against the ridge, howling and shrieking up the stone face. Both man flattened against the rock and dug their hands into the crevices. When the wind died down, they began climbing down the stone tiers.

Sea spray and rain had painted slick shadows across the sheer facade, making their progress treacherous. They moved slowly, using grappling hooks, ropes and determined willpower.

Finally they reached the lowest shelf of rock, which loomed about twenty yards above the thrashing waves and extended like a splintery walkway toward a thick grove of trees. Like men on a high-wire, they treaded softly but steadily along the walkway until they reached the edge of the forest. Once inside the safety of the shadows, they moved quickly.

They followed a course parallel to the coastline, never too far from the hiss and roar of the ocean. Then, at the end of a boulder-strewn spearhead of land, Haimyo flashed a beacon out to sea where a Maritime Self-Defense Force "fishing boat" waited for their signal.

Soon they saw its black silhouette cresting the waves.

And though they couldn't see it in the dark, they knew that a few miles farther out a Japanese Haruna Class destroyer knifed through the waters, conducting maneuvers along the eastern rim of Hokkaido. On board were three Sikorsky SH-3 helicopters, each capable of transporting more than thirty commandos.

Though Kuro had been implicated in the clan killings, as yet there was no clear proof of his involvement. There were no defectors from the sect, and none of the fallen clansmen at the hotel skirmish had survived to face interrogation.

The same held true for Yukiko. Her appearance at the hotel hit was only conjecture. She'd worn a wig and had disguised herself well. No matter how correct their hunch was that the woman had led the attack force, hunches weren't enough to bring her before a court of law.

No, Bolan thought, a more primitive law was at work on the island. A law he'd soon enforce.

PHANTOMS HOWLED in the stream of wind that wound around Kuro's glass-walled redoubt like a cold noose.

A chorus of angry souls chattered endlessly at the leader of the Unseen Powers, the voices of the fallen warriors, the champions he'd counted on to rid him of his enemies.

Their deaths were in vain.

There were no victories, no rejoicing. Only sorrow and hatred. There'd be no paintings or scrolls to commemorate the great deeds of Kuro's clan. They'd suffered defeat after defeat at the hands of Mako Tamura and the Executioner. The American and the defector were the true Unseen Powers, ahead of the clan every step of the way.

The proof was right in front of him in living color. Glowing faces beamed down into the room from a large backlit projection screen. They flickered above him like Technicolor apparitions as videotaped news reports of the troubles besetting the Unseen Powers played one after the other on the screen.

Yukiko sat motionless behind him, entranced in grim fascination by the parade of news clips. It was like watching an autopsy of the clan.

On-screen an attractive young network reporter was standing in front of the hotel where the JEICO conference had been held. Her breathless voice and her photogenic smile made it sound as if she were conducting a tour.

"Until the massacre at this hotel, U.P. Kobudo was considered one of Japan's model new religions. But according to some highly placed government officials, the gunmen who tried to kidnap Saburo Watanabe and began indiscriminately shooting at innocent party-goers have been linked to the sect."

The scene shifted from the hotel to a picture of Yamishima, then to a photograph of Taro Kuro

walking outside of his home. The high-resolution shot
had been taken from above.

"Satellites," Kuro said. "Now they're using satellites against me. The Americans have keyhole satellites that can practically take pictures of your soul."

"A measure of your power," Yukiko said, "that
shows how much they fear you."

"Perhaps. Or perhaps it shows the lengths they'll go
to destroy me."

Several more pictures flashed on the screen, showing the elegant house surrounded by ponds and gardens. The reporter's voice continued. "Taro Kuro lives
in luxury at his palatial estate on Yamishima, an island he commands his followers to call Kamishima.
The leader of the sect has denied all involvement with
any of the criminal activities that have rocked Japan."

The next photo showed a brochure-style picture of
Takahashi's hot-springs resort. "However, this idyl-
lic paradise in Hakone was run by an associate of the
sect leader." The next photograph showed the after-
math of the battle at the hot springs, with the bodies
of the clansmen littering the landscape. "Gang warfare destroyed the resort and took the lives of several
clan members. Authorities surmise that an underworld war is being fought to gain control of criminal
enterprises in Tokyo, many of them rumored to be run
from this establishment."

Strategically filmed topless dancers from Club Scandinavia paraded on-screen, followed by a close-up of the neon sign in front. "The club had been linked to underworld activity and, through a series of shell corporations, to the sect itself."

The litany continued as footage from several different reports cataloged the series of crimes and murders linked to the Unseen Powers. The media had played up the story big. Nihon TV, Tokyo Broadcasting Service and Fuji TV all carried stories on the sect.

Tabloid papers and radio news networks had milked the story for all it was worth. The Unseen Powers were much too visible for a supposedly secret society, Kuro knew. The clan wouldn't tolerate it much longer. He had to bring the challenge to an honorable end.

If the media didn't cannibalize him first, he thought, as he listened to the damning voices of the reporters.

"...A samurai soap opera where the players are murderous thugs..."

"...Nothing but thieves and murderers hiding under a patriotic flag, a religious cult with a dogma of death and destruction..."

"...Ever since his brother, Ieyasu Kuro, was killed in a mysterious incident that some authorities claim was related to extortionate demands made on the JEICO project, there has been an ever-increasing spiral of violence..."

The indictment by media was nearly all one-sided. But at the end of the taped news reports, Kuro had included the one favorable view of the sect. The reporter had been co-opted by the Unseen Powers long ago and had filmed Kuro's responses during a clandestine stopover in Tokyo.

He looked with pleasure as his beatific face appeared on the screen, savoring his own words as they echoed back at him. "The American presence in Japan rightly concerns us all, particularly when it comes to military and Intelligence operations conducted against innocent people. The attacks on our religious society have the marks of a typical disinformation campaign, blaming the crimes of others on us. I believe it's masterful propaganda and nothing more, created by a conspiracy of American and Japanese gangsters."

The reporter nodded, then asked a series of questions that Kuro had provided beforehand. The sincere face of Taro Kuro beamed at the audience once again as he continued speaking. "I'm a religious man, and that means there are certain constraints on me. But I can pray for vengeance, and for guidance. In the meantime the Unseen Powers will see to the wives and children of all those who have been martyred by these common criminals. As for those false accusations about links between killers and the Unseen Powers, I wish to make it clear that we denounce violence in all of its forms. If some misguided associates of the sect commit crimes, then I'll be the first to call for their punishment.''

The news clip ended with Kuro's regal glance at the camera.

"Pity the poor holy man," Yukiko said. "Besieged at his own shrine."

He glanced sideways at her. "A siege we must break."

"How?"

"Our own counsel is dead," he said. "Void. We must contact the spirits again."

She blanched, but then she nodded her agreement. Despite the risk, there was no other choice. They had to summon the Unseen Powers themselves.

As if a part of her had known beforehand, she was dressed in a black silk robe that clung to her body, shifting slightly like a movable skin. The color of night, decorated with silver and gold figures along the seams, it gave her an ethereal poise.

Kuro turned off the projection screen, dimmed the lights and struck a match. Next he lit the candles and ceremonial lanterns that cast a soothing glow upon the room.

With each passing moment they discarded their earthbound identities and opened themselves up to the powers around them.

They moved to a corner of the room where a gods' shelf awaited them. Scrolls hung from the wall, bearing secret and sacred histories of their ancestors. Beneath images of gods painted by Yukiko were several small strips of rolled paper, written prayers to the Unseen Powers.

Kuro positioned a large brass bowl between himself and his companion as they sat on thin straw mats. He dropped the rolled prayers inside the bowl and gradually fashioned them into a pyre. He torched them, filling the air with ink-stained incense.

The sect leader then began to chant, his cadence a dim echo trailing behind Yukiko's throaty murmurings.

The woman drifted rapidly into a trance. She was the *nakaze,* the medium whose thoughts drifted with the smoke. She had already summoned the sleeping spirits that swam in the dark seas of the mind.

And they came to her.

Her body stiffened as she knelt before the pantheon of gods, a gasp of pain, of surprise, the only prayer upon her lips.

And then her eyes opened.

"The American is here," she announced.

Kuro looked away from her eyes. Though he knew it was impossible for the American to be on Yamishima, he wasn't about to deny the conviction that burned like embers in her brutal gaze.

He glanced around the room, then peered through the windows out at the night.

"He's not here."

A hiss burned from her lips. "He is." Her voice was deep and raspy as if her own identity had been wrapped and enfolded by someone else's, by one of the gods who screamed in the night wind. "I can sense him now. He watches, and he waits."

As if they had a mind of their own, Kuro's hands waved in the air, his fingers curled like claws, trying to track the presence of the American. But the Executioner wasn't easy prey.

If indeed the man was here, Kuro couldn't sense him. Not completely. Not with the rational part of his mind. But the part of his mind that was in sync with the sorceress was able to visualize the American, almost seeing his spirit enveloping the island.

But it wasn't real, Kuro thought. This was madness. Yukiko was mad, and he, too, had stepped past the boundaries of reason.

But Kuro quickly buried the heretical thought. When the gods were manifest, it was best not to let them hear the doubt echoing in his mind.

Yukiko suddenly snapped her head to the left and gazed straight at Kuro. Her nipples were erect now, pushing at the silk that draped her flesh like a flag of passion. Her lips moved slowly, but she uttered no sound. Then her teeth bit down sharply and caused her to gasp out loud. A fleck of blood appeared on her lips.

Kuro recoiled.

"What is it?" he asked, worry seeping into his words. He wasn't afraid of men, but the angry spirits of the warriors he'd sent to their deaths were a different matter. And it was their voices, all of them condensed into one entity, that spoke through Yukiko's lips. He blotted out the fright in his voice and forced himself to confront the spirits inhabiting the goddess. "What's wrong?"

"The man who walks with death walks close to us."

Lantern light flickered above them as if there were wind in the room. The spirits had somehow seeped through the cracks in the seams of Kuro's house.

"The man who walks with death must be led down another path," she said.

It was an endless path, Kuro thought, one that always wound back to his place. The American would come. But if the gods wanted it, he wouldn't stand in the way. He listened to the voice of Yukiko and to the minds of the gods, even though he thought the American would still come.

"The girl must die," Yukiko said suddenly. "She's the prize our enemies want. She's the one who whispers our secrets to them. Take her and make sure that she never returns. And it will lead our enemies away from us."

"Which girl?" Kuro asked.

"The blonde at the club."

He laughed. "They're all blond."

Yukiko's face hardened into a mask of silent fury. "The blonde who betrayed us. The one who even now is preparing to leave."

Now he knew which one she was talking of. One of the dancers was almost free from the clan. Negotiations for her services were almost complete.

It made sense, Kuro thought. They knew there had been leaks coming from the club. There was no guarantee that they'd purged all the traitors from their ranks, but he couldn't help but wonder how much of this desire to find a scapegoat came from the goddess and how much stemmed from Yukiko's natural jealousy of a rival.

The girl could be useful. If indeed she was cooperating with Tamura, then she could be used as a diversion. He could have her removed from the club, held hostage to keep Tamura and his Executioner at bay.... Interrogate her.... It could be more than useful, he thought. It could be entertaining.

But now another type of entertainment was at hand.

Yukiko's eyes were veiled with a mist of lust as she returned from the trance. She dropped to the floor beside him, shuddering and covered with sweat— waiting to be possessed by her lover....

CLUB SCANDINAVIA was alive, Sandra Valcour thought as the walls of her dressing room vibrated and thumped from the heavy bass lines of the jukebox.

The dim sound of laughter and clinking glasses infiltrated through the supposedly soundproof walls.

She'd just left the stage, her place taken by another "Nordic" stripper. Soon the stage would be behind her forever. But first she had to finish her last night. It was typical of the clan. The smiling vultures squeezed everything they could from you, right up to the moment they didn't own you anymore.

That moment would come tonight.

Mako Tamura was pulling her out at last. Only one more show remained.

She sat in front of the makeup mirror, her reflection enshrined by a halo of light bulbs. The high-cheeked face looking back at her was still beautiful— on the outside, at least.

Inside, she was ravaged. The years had taken their toll on her spirit. Unless she escaped her Kabukicho cage, the inside desolation would catch up with the outside. Then she'd topple even further from the tawdry pinnacle of Club Scandinavia with all its phony Nordic dancers.

Despite the harsh life she led here, she knew there were worse places to work.

It was all such a charade, she thought. Right down to the gaudy golden breastplates that exaggerated her cleavage and made her "Ride of the Valkyries" act such a hit with the customers.

And the golden tiara that was supposed to transform her into an exotic Viking queen was tinsel-topped cardboard that made her look like some kind of Wonder Woman gone wrong. Even her tan lines were artificial, courtesy of hours spent in a tanning salon.

But it was ending soon.

The man who was getting her out had been sitting in the audience tonight. The Security Bureau agent was posing as an underworld figure who'd bought out her contract from the clan. Since girls were bought, sold and traded like cattle in the underworld, the clan considered it business as usual. Plus they got a good price for her.

It was a fair exchange, she thought. The information she'd been feeding to Tamura was worth a small fortune.

She sipped from a long-stemmed glass of wine, her constant companion over the years. Booze and barbituates had taken the place of people she could trust. Some dancers used even harder stuff to blot out the day-to-day struggle of life under the clan. And naturally the clan always had a plentiful supply on hand.

Like most of the dancers at the club, Sandra had been blinded by stars in her eyes when she had signed on with the "dancing troupe" scheduled to tour the Orient. After years of knocking on the doors of Hollywood studios and, more often then not, landing on her back, it had seemed like a dream come true.

But the dream quickly turned into a nightmare.

When they reached Japan, the women who'd been promised show business careers ended up showing their bodies in strip clubs and peddling them to the customers. Their main incentive was a chance to keep on living if they obeyed their new "talent managers."

Fear was the invisible chain that held them all together. Separated from their friends in a foreign land, divided up like spoils of war, the girls were ruled by harsh underworld clansmen who thought nothing of maiming or killing women who tried to get away.

For most of them the only way out was to be bought out or buried. Or they could try to go to the authorities. But perversely enough, the clan made it a point of honor to hunt down the women. Sooner or later they always caught them.

Sandra had planned her escape early on. While most of the girls had learned bedroom Japanese, she worked hard at mastering the language and never let on just how much she understood. The clansmen thought she was just empty-headed fluff, which gave her entry into places where she could overhear privileged conversations.

Eventually she struck pay dirt and managed to pass some valuable information to the authorities. Tamura caught her case and from that moment on had groomed and coached her in the informant game. She'd done more than her part, and now it was time for her debut as a free woman.

Suddenly the music got louder, and so did the noise of the nightclub. It was only a sliver of amplified sound. Whoever entered the room had closed the door quickly behind them.

She turned slightly and froze when she saw her guests. The first one was the Japanese man, Iwai Kobayushi, who wore his customary shades and a black suit. His presence scared her. He came around only when something was wrong—something dead wrong.

"What's going on?" she asked.

Kobayushi ignored her and stepped to the side of the room. Then he nodded at the second man, a hulking blond-haired American who worked for the clan. His name was Underwood, though the clansman had nicknamed him "Undertaker." The last time she'd seen him was in the company of two clansmen who'd disappeared forever.

She summoned all the indignation she could muster and shouted, "Now look—"

Underwood's hand sealed her mouth just as easily as he could seal her fate. His sweaty callused palm closed tightly around her chin and turned her head back to the mirror. Cartilage snapped loudly from the motion, a foreshadow of things to come.

"No, doll," Underwood said, "you look." He dropped his hands to her shoulders, slowly massaging them at first, but then gradually increasing the pressure and pushing her down in the chair.

Simian hands, she thought, watching the huge knuckles whiten even further.

Then they moved toward her throat.

She clawed at his hands, but they were like iron clamps locked around her neck.

The pain came slowly but grew more intense as the flow of air to her brain was cut off. Hammers pounded inside her skull, and her chest strained from the pressure.

Just when she thought she was going to black out, he released her, and a sick thought struck her. He was familiar with this kind of routine, knew where the thresholds of pain were and how best to reach them, how to loiter around them and bring his victims to the breaking point.

She massaged her throat and gently moved her neck from side to side. Gasping a few times from the effort to talk, she reached out for the wineglass. It tasted like nectar as it washed away the pain. Finally her voice returned. "What's the matter?" she said. "What've I done?"

"Nothing's the matter," he replied. "Nothing that can't be fixed. As far as what you've done . . . you've done too much."

"I'm supposed to get out tonight," she said. "Someone's made a mistake."

"Uh-huh, doll. And it's you. You're on center stage night." He sounded amused; he was starting to enjoy himself. One look at his feral grin, and she knew she wouldn't get out. Not from the club. Not from this room.

This was her last performance.

"We checked out the man who wants to buy your contract," Underwood told her. "He's not who he says he is."

"I don't know who he is—"

"We think you do. We think you know a lot about him and his friends. As a matter of fact we think you've been telling him all about the clan."

Underwood looked over at Kobayushi. The clansman had stood there impassively. Now he gave the enforcer an imperceptible nod.

The hardman gripped her shoulders once again. Then his hands crept over her skin and moved slowly toward her neck. "Now's the time, doll," he said. "Who are they, and what have you told them?"

He was a trainer, she thought, someone who broke down the girls when they first arrived. And he was an enforcer who carried out the laws of the clan. That meant that sooner or later she'd be carried out. Dead and cold.

In her mind Sandra saw herself picking up the wineglass and smashing it into his face. Then she could run past him and . . . And nothing. It was only a fantasy, like everything else in the club. He'd catch her and it would be worse.

His hands gripped her neck.

Suddenly she heard a crashing and shuddering sound, and the loud roar of music and clapping filled the room.

Only part of her mind registered why sound had boomed into the room all of a sudden.

The door was off its hinges.

A clansman was flying backward into the room, landing on the floor unconscious as it dropped beneath him, sliding across the floor like a surfboard.

Two men charged into the room after him.

MACK BOLAN TOUCHED DOWN on the floor with his right foot, then launched himself at the Japanese man who was reaching into his suitcoat for a gun. The Executioner caught him halfway with a side thrust kick, the blow pinning his arm against his holster and knocking him back against the wall.

Bolan braced himself, swung his hips forward and put full power into a palm-heel strike with his left hand. The loud smack stunned Kobayushi's forehead as he rebounded from the wall, and he dropped to the ground like a rag doll.

Tamura concentrated on Underwood, reaching out for him as the blond-haired giant hesitated with his hands just inches away from the girl. The enforcer was figuring out the best person to attack—Tamura or the girl.

The girl made up his mind for him, smashing his face with the wineglass. She put years of repressed fury into the blow, pushing up so hard the glass broke and a claw-shaped spear of glass gouged into his flesh.

She twisted savagely as if she were trying to core an apple.

He bellowed and stepped up and away from the attack, leaving a geyser of blood behind.

Tamura rapped him once in the kidney with a half fist, the folded knuckles cutting him down like an ax. When Underwood collapsed to his knees, the security chief methodically put him down for keeps with a side kick to the jaw that levered him flat out on the floor.

Tamura's backup man stood in the doorway, his Nambu automatic searching the room for a target. But everything was already under control.

On the other side of the room Bolan had disarmed Kobayushi. For the moment he kept him on the floor, the Beretta pointed at his head.

Now that the chaos had stopped, Sandra bolted from the chair. "Oh, God," she said, grabbing at Tamura. "Thanks. He was going to... He was going to..."

"We know what he was here for." The security chief glanced behind him at his backup man. "You can thank Haimyo for alerting us. We were waiting outside, but as soon as he saw the Undertaker, he called us in. It wasn't too hard to guess they'd found you out."

As if on cue, Underwood groaned and tried to sit up. He made it halfway, then shook his head from side to side. Rivulets of blood cascaded from his gashed cheek.

Tamura stepped closer to him and said, "You weren't part of the deal."

Kobayushi stirred from the other side of the room. "Neither were you," he said. Disheveled and disoriented, he was shaking off the effects of the Executioner's lightning blitz. Bolan motioned with the gun and let him sit up.

The security chief shrugged. "Then I suggest we make a new deal. We're prepared to be reasonable."

"I'm a realist," Kobayushi replied. "I'll listen and I'll live."

"All right. Here's the deal. Tonight we were going to bring Sandra out, even give you a little payment. But that's over now. The new deal is that you get a bullet if anyone looks cross-eyed at her. From here on in she's under my protection. If anything happens to her, your whole house comes down. Every last clansman will fall. Understand?"

"Understood." Kobayushi's face revealed his relief that he could walk away from this. Under the circumstances he could have easily been silenced forever. But obviously there was something else that had to be straightened out. He looked up at the Executioner. "What are you doing here?"

"I was in the neighborhood. This used to be the place I came to find the clan's champions. But it looks like you're running out of them. Or maybe you're just running out."

"Our champions await you."

"Right. Are you one of them?"

Kobayushi fell silent.

"Didn't think so," Bolan replied, studying the man's face. "But you do look familiar. Stand up."

With a studied slowness, the clansman got to his feet.

"You fit the description of one of the gunmen at the hotel," Bolan said. He looked at the dark sunglasses that had been knocked onto the floor. "Right down to your shades."

"We all look alike to *gajin*. Your incompetence isn't our problem."

"Maybe," Bolan replied. "But I'll tell you what *is* your problem. The clan challenged me to combat, but then they suddenly grew quiet. They've either taken up the peace pipe, or there's no one left to face me."

Kobayushi stared back at him. "You seem to know a lot about us. You tell me."

"I'll tell you this. Unless another champion is named by this time tomorrow, tell Kuro I'll assume he's last champion."

"And?"

"Tell him I'm coming to kill him and anyone who stands in my way."

Kobayushi recoiled as he saw the future of the clan written in the Executioner's eyes.

"I'll see you there," Bolan promised.

10

Korin Sato waited in the cedar shadows that shielded his traditional wood-and-tile home from the hot afternoon sun. Tall trees flanked the house on both sides, naturally camouflaging it with the thick woods that bristled along the western coast of Hokkaido.

He sat on the soft grass in front of his house, brewing tea atop a small platform campfire. The wood had turned to embers long ago, wafting a strong scent in the air.

Sato lived close enough to the city of Sapporo to attend to clan affairs whenever he was needed. But he spent most of his time here at his secluded haven fifty miles southwest of Sapporo on a wild stretch of Uchiura Bay. Keeping him company was a mistress half his age who took care of all the earthly needs of a man in his position.

A champion.

He'd been waiting calmly ever since the clan had delivered the latest challenge to the American. Despite the clan chieftain's bold words of encouragement to him, Sato knew the man was faltering. Taro

Kuro was afraid, afraid that the American would cut through them all. Each champion's death was like a sword cut to Kuro himself, slowly bleeding him to death.

Perhaps, Sato thought, perhaps not.

Soon he'd know.

The American was on the trail even now. Umeyo had run fawnlike through the forest from her vantage point where she'd been watching the trail below.

"He comes, he comes," she'd said, as if it was a great day for them, another secret chapter about to be written in the book of the Unseen Powers.

"I've seen him."

"But you haven't moved from this spot," she'd protested.

"I've seen him through your eyes, Umeyo. And now you must hide so he doesn't see you."

The young woman had stepped back into the woods. Now he could sense her eyes peeking fearfully from the bowers. The eyes of Umeyo, he thought. They would tell the tale.

It was amusing in a way. She'd be the only one from the clan to see the American in combat. The chieftain had wanted to seed the forest with warriors who would end the American's trail with a hundred arrows, but Sato had forbidden it.

Even if Taro Kuro was no longer a fit chieftain, even if the clan was no longer a fit society, Korin Sato was still a champion. A true warrior didn't hide in the shadows. Especially when it involved a matter of honor.

THE BLACK-CLAD Executioner came upon a girl who crouched at the edge of the woods. She was unarmed, a noncombatant.

Perhaps his opponent had sent her here for safe-keeping, he thought. A daughter? A wife? The answer didn't matter. Whoever she was, she was a part of the clan and obviously knew he was coming.

He knew he could have been spotted earlier on a brief open stretch of the lower trail. That couldn't be helped. He'd crossed the clearing quickly before drifting into cover once again to carry out his recon.

He'd studied the layout of Sato's house long enough to know there was no one else around but the two of them. The only sound was the occasional rush of warm wind through the trees and the distant roar of waves breaking on rocks.

No assassins crouched in hiding. There appeared to be no trickery this time.

Bolan soundlessly circled back to the trail and followed it to a thin dirt walkway that coiled around the front of the house.

The clansman waited for him in a Buddha-like pose, sitting undisturbed on the grass. Though the top of his head was bald, there were thatches of jet black hair ringing his skull like a crown. He was in his midforties and heavily muscled beneath a taut black T-shirt.

"Korin Sato?"

"Hai," the man replied. Then, as if he were carefully thinking out each word, he spoke in slow but precise English. "That is my name."

Bolan unslung his pack and dropped it to the ground. It carried several extra magazines for the Beretta, which was holstered in an underarm rig. It also carried rations and survival gear in case he had an indefinite stay on the island.

It may as well have carried feathers for all the attention the other man paid to it. He looked so unconcerned at his presence that Bolan repeated his name. "Korin Sato."

"Yes."

"You know why I'm here."

The man stared straight ahead.

"I've come to kill you," Bolan said.

Sato reached for the cup of tea sitting on a square-shaped rock to his left. He sipped slowly, then stirred the cup as if the leaves held his fortune. "We share the same objective," he said, setting the cup back down.

Then Sato rose to his feet in one fluid motion, lightly springing up on his heels. He faced Bolan squarely. No longer was he a placid soul.

A lesser man would have been lost in the dark gaze of his depthless eyes, intimidated by the will that lurked within. But Bolan had seen the look before. He'd also used it himself from time to time.

Many *karate-ka* used a similar technique to unnerve their opponents, either looking into the other man's eyes as if they were transparent or staring at the man's breastbone as though it was an inanimate target about to be shattered by a greater force. It gave the opponent the impression he was facing an unstoppable killing machine.

But machines could fail, especially if they were made of flesh and blood.

"There's no need to die for Kuro," Bolan said.

"Of course," Sato replied. "You can turn around and go home now."

"My road takes me to Kuro."

"Then your road ends here."

"What kind of weapons?" Bolan asked.

Sato spoke slowly. "One man may favor the sword. Another the staff. Still another the dagger. But there is always the chance of an unequal combat. A true warrior relies only upon the weapons he was born with. Is that satisfactory?"

"It is."

"Then it begins." Sato bowed curtly, then he exploded in fury, leaping high and landing in a horse stance directly in front of Bolan. His left hand darted for the warrior's temple, requiring a countering block from the Executioner's right.

The Japanese grabbed on to Bolan's hand for leverage, tugging it forward as his left foot slapped the earth. At the same time his right foot pistoned forward in a straightforward snap kick.

The blunt strike would have crushed Bolan's groin if it had hit full force. He stepped back, turned his right foot inward and tensed his leg muscles. His rigid thigh caught the blow, then relaxed immediately after contact to spread out and dilute the impact.

His body went on autopilot. Slightly off balance, he went in the direction Sato was pulling. Closing with him, Bolan spun to his left so he was back-to-back with the clansman and whipped an elbow into his spine.

There was a loud thud, and Sato jumped as if he'd been hit with a bolt of electricity.

The Executioner completed the circle until he was in front of him. His hands flew toward Sato's face. He cupped one hand under the man's chin and pushed sharply at the back of his head, intent on breaking his neck.

Sato recovered in time to turn with the motion. His praying-mantis hands speared upward and broke Bolan's grip, then clawed for his eyes.

Bolan moved to the right and countered with a two-handed strike, his fists snapping shut like pincers toward the sides of Sato's head. The clansman had to pull back—that, or have his skull crushed.

Both men faced each other, taking deep long breaths. Less than a minute had passed, and already they were past the edge. Civilization was a memory. A luxury that neither man could afford.

There were no niceties. Every move was designed to finish off the opponent. It was winner-take-all and the prize was life.

Sato's right foot whirled out in a crescent kick. Bolan stepped into it, blocking the kick with his right hand, kneeing his opponent in the groin and dropping a hammerfist to his chest.

The sturdy clansman landed on his back but moved the moment he touched the earth, pushing himself up and away from Bolan's kill strike. The warrior's fist hit nothing but air while Sato scrambled away and got to his feet.

Pressing the attack, the Executioner jumped in the air, left foot slicing the air in a fake kick that pulled back at the last instant, while his right foot shot toward Sato's chest and caught him just under the ribs.

As Bolan closed in again, the Japanese rocketed out with a side kick to his left shoulder that stunned him for a long and dangerous moment.

A burst of pain ran down the warrior's arm and made his fingers fall open. It felt as if he'd been hit with a wooden club. His arm was useless as Sato struck first with his fist, then with his foot, hitting Bolan in the upper body and positioning him for the kill.

A roundhouse kick axed toward his head.

Bolan ducked, instinctively hurtling forward. He had to counter quickly with his good right hand or he was dead. He pulled back his fingers in a rigid claw, then struck Sato's forehead with the rigid edge of his palm.

It gave him a second to follow through. As Sato's head snapped back, Bolan's hand twisted around in a blur, his knuckles cutting across the man's eyes. He felt water and blood jump onto his hand.

Sato struck out blindly, his ham fists crashing into Bolan's shoulder. But the Executioner ignored the pain. Instead, he continued the attack, his hand snapping into his opponent's already bruised forehead. There was a crack of imploding bone as part of his skull caved in like a third eye awakening.

Suspended between life and death, the clansman charged, wanting to die as a warrior and perhaps kill one more time.

Bolan clotheslined him.

His pain-racked left arm swept around the back of Sato's neck while his right forearm hammered into the front. They clinched together on his throat.

Sato fell backward onto the ground like cut timber.

It was over.

The champion was dead.

A few moments later Bolan heard a rustling sound near the forest. The girl stepped out from the trees in a daze, moving slowly toward the fallen clansman with hypnotic funereal grace.

Then she knelt next to him.

"There was no other way," Bolan told her.

She looked up at the Executioner and spoke a few harsh words in Japanese that he didn't catch. But he understood the language of the eyes. She, too, had known there was no other way out for either of the warriors. They'd each made their choices long before they met in combat.

Bolan turned and headed back down the trail.

Now the only champions who stood in his way were the ones on the island.

It was time to make a pilgrimage.

11

"Korin Sato is dead," Haruki announced.

Taro Kuro sat at the head of the small circle of clansmen who had met at his hilltop home for the customary tea ceremony that had preceded their council. It was a strained meeting. Word had spread fast around the island. Another champion had fallen. So had Kuro's prestige.

And now the sage was making trouble.

"In war we must be ready to make sacrifices," Kuro said. "It has always been that way."

"Sacrifices, yes," the sage replied. "Mistakes, no. Too many lives have been thrown away."

Kuro glared at the silver-haired man. "You've been asked because of your past position, not your present."

"Akira Takahashi is dead," the sage pressed, ignoring the reprimand. He knew he hadn't been asked to join the council out of kindness or the vestiges of respect due a man of his position. The other clansmen had insisted that he be allowed to attend the meeting.

According to the rules of the clan, everyone had a chance to speak during the councils. Since this might be the last gathering of the Unseen Powers, he wasn't going to be a silent observer. Instead, he voiced the strongest and simplest argument against Kuro's leadership. The facts. "Naoto is dead."

Kuro looked from face to face. The hard-eyed men looked straight ahead, none condemning the sage. Other than Iwai Kobayushi, none of them openly embraced Kuro's position.

Sitting to his right, Kobayushi fixed the sage with a stare that said he'd be glad to add yet another name to the list of the dead.

Haruki continued naming the names, though not out of sympathy with their plight. Most of them deserved to die. It was like a cleansing of the clan. But the recital of their deaths could help sway the clansmen who were leaning toward a return of the old ways, to a time when the Unseen Powers weren't a band of brigands.

"Ieyasu is dead," the sage continued, "as is Jiro."

There were low murmurs from the group. Jiro had attained an almost mythical status among the clan. Despite his slender scarecrow frame, Jiro had bested all of the warriors in combat. He'd been the one brought into action whenever the clan was in trouble and needed someone who could pull them out.

But no longer would he be by their side.

"I was there when Jiro fell," Kobayushi said. "He was doing what the gods said."

"No," the older man contradicted, "Jiro was doing what the sorceress said. He gave his life for us, Iwai. Yet you returned. You and that witch Yukiko. She had led us all astray. And where is she now?"

"She speaks with the gods even now," Kuro replied.

An uneasy silence fell over the clansmen. By now the pattern was clear. Whenever Yukiko sought counsel from the Unseen Powers, more clansmen would fall.

"She speaks with the wrong gods," the sage said. "She speaks with gods of vengeance, not of victory. She speaks with spirits who rob us of our soul."

"Enough!" Kuro shouted, his right hand slashing the air like a scepter.

Haruki stopped talking. He'd made his point. He'd sowed doubt about their leader in the minds of the clansmen. In the beginning Kuro had been the one closest to the gods. Things had gone wrong ever since the American had come on the scene, ever since the challenge had been issued to him—ever since Kuro had turned to his mistress for her celestial counsel.

"You're very good at naming names and telling tales of woe, old man. But what's your solution?"

"It's very simple," he replied. "The gods don't want the champions to die."

"What do they want?"

"The gods want the contest ended. Here." The sage brought his arm down sharply, his knife hand cutting the air. Then the old man pointed at Kuro. "It falls on your head. You're the only champion who needs to fight."

Kuro's face reddened. Not from fear, but anger. And it wasn't directed solely at Haruki's insolence. It was directed at the clansmen who sat and listened to the old man without shouting him down, without standing up for Kuro.

"The American is coming," Kuro said, "and he'll be met by a champion of the clan."

"Yourself?" the sage asked.

"In time."

"I see. Then the American can expect to find more dishonorable men waiting for him. He accepted the sacred challenge from the clan, and we've blackened that challenge with our deceit. With ambushes. With common gunmen. And that is why the Unseen Powers have turned against us."

Kuro exhaled loudly as he turned his cutting gaze once more on the sage. Leaning forward, he said, "Perhaps they aren't the ones who've turned against us, old man. Perhaps the poison comes from another source. Rest assured, whoever has betrayed us will be punished."

The council continued, then, and one by one the clansmen cast their votes on how to deal with the American.

Two NIGHTS LATER the Executioner crept up the Yamishima ridge once more. Ascending the rocky gray staircase with him was Haimyo.

"It's clear," Bolan said after scanning the woods with the thermal imager.

In their night black garb, they filtered through the edge of the woods and waited in the darkness for the approach of Haruki.

Landing on the island unnoticed wasn't that great a task for experienced men like Bolan and Haimyo. But carrying out the attack and getting off the island in one piece required a lot of preparation.

In fact, this time around it required the help of the gods themselves. Or at least the illusion of their help.

Twenty minutes passed before they saw Haruki drifting along the borderline of shadows, his walking stick tamping the ground in front of him. He glided across a small clearing, his silver hair glowing in the splinter of moonlight. Then he stopped suddenly as if he were looking out to sea.

But his senses were looking all around him.

Finally the sage turned toward the woods where Bolan and Haimyo waited. He joined them in the shadows and spoke briefly to Haimyo before the security man drifted off into the woods, moving uphill to guard against any wandering clansmen.

Then he looked up at the Executioner. "They know you're coming."

"Yeah," Bolan replied, "but not when or how."

Haruki nodded. "When last we met, you mentioned the use of magic. Am I to believe that now you consult the Unseen Powers?"

Bolan shook his head. "My magic comes direct from Uncle Sam's pharmacy." He opened a leather pouch containing several glassine-wrapped parcels of wheat-colored powder.

The narcotic mixture had been delivered to him courtesy of the CIA's technical services outfit, which was a fancy name for their dirty tricks brigade. The drug would have a delayed knockout effect, and it wouldn't be fatal. "The next tea party's on me," the warrior said, then explained how the powder had to be prepared.

After questioning Bolan about the dosages, Haruki briefed him on the preparations of the clan. Not only were they expecting him to come, but they also expected to stop him before he even set foot on the island. Following Kuro's orders, Iwai Kobayushi had commandeered a small fleet of fishing boats that scoured the waters, looking for the seaward approach of the Executioner.

"We know," Bolan said. "We've seen them. So far we've managed to avoid them at night."

"There are other clansmen about. The spirits of the slain ones are also watching for you."

The ghost guard, Bolan thought. But the phantoms hadn't packed much of a punch so far. After all, they'd managed to infiltrate the island several times without incident. But the Executioner didn't mock the sage's beliefs. "I'll trust in you to keep them at bay, Grandfather."

The sage nodded. "And I'll trust you not to swell their ranks with new souls."

Bolan nodded. He knew that the sage had pressed Haimyo about his American ways, and Haimyo had assured him that Bolan wasn't a deranged mercenary, that he was interested in a surgical strike instead of a bloodbath. Haimyo's claims bolstered the sage's own impressions. Unless he trusted both men implicitly, he couldn't hope to salvage the clan.

Their aim was the same—to rid the clan of the murderous disciples of Taro Kuro. The Executioner went over the details one more time, making sure that Haruki would be ready by the time he launched his attack. Then he said, "It's up to us now, Grandfather."

"And to the gods," the man replied.

THE RUSTED HULL of the fishing trawler knifed through the windswept waters of the Pacific shortly before dawn. Like a splinter skinning under the surging waves, it shot straight for the harbor.

A sprinkling of lights shone from shuttered windows on shore, but most of the island was still in darkness. The night was lifting slowly.

So was the bitter wind.

The storm drowned out the roar and throbbing of the engine as the boat headed for the secluded harbor. Pelting rain and towering waves battered at the aging fishing boat.

Inside the wheelhouse the captain of the ship looked through sightless eyes at the rocky shore.

His right hand held an automatic pistol in his lap, his dead white fingers clenched in a futile grip. He was still sitting in his chair, looking as if he were planning on sailing the ship into the afterlife.

One shot had nailed him.

Behind him one of his crewmen was sprawled on his back near the door where a pool of red coated the floorboards. A jagged crimson collar blossomed around his neck like a grim blueprint of his execution by garrote.

His holster flap was unsnapped, but his 9 mm automatic remained sheathed in leather. Though he'd gone for his weapon, the thin wire looped around his throat had changed his mind. The clansman had tried to paw at the garrote, but by then it was too late. In practiced hands death by garrote came quick.

The man who was now at the ship's wheel had years of practice. Bolan had sailed this kind of course before.

His eyes watched the distant shore through a shifting mist. Sea spray shrouded the windows and curtained off the islands from view. From time to time the Executioner glanced behind him. It was habit more than not, but it was habit that had kept him from joining the silent passengers in the wheelhouse.

They weren't the only ones who'd abandoned ship forever.

Below decks the rest of the crew was in the same shape. Two were riddled with automatic fire from the Beretta 93-R. Chunks of wood gouged from the cabin walls showed the zigzag path their own lethal sprays of lead had taken. But their submachine guns had been fired wildly. They had been in a state of shock when Bolan had stepped into their midst and opened up with two 3-round bursts. One, two. They were out for good.

On the deck outside the wheelhouse lay another body.

Iwai Kobayushi. His postponed death had finally caught up with him.

Kobayushi had run out onto the deck during the middle of the battle. Like his men, he'd awakened to find himself locked in a death struggle with the very man they searched the seas for.

And the clansmen had fallen left and right. Precise bursts from the Beretta had cut through their wild firing as Bolan had moved from cabin to cabin on a lethal search and destroy, changing 9 mm clips on the run.

Kobayushi had heard the gunfire all around him, but the site of the hits moved so fast that he couldn't zero in on the black-clad Executioner. Until finally only Kobayushi remained on deck.

And the sounds stopped.

He'd stood there with an automatic rifle in his hand, whirling slowly in circles with the long barrel looking about for the shape of death that moved in the shadows of the ship.

Bolan had walked alongside the wheelhouse, stopping just twenty feet from the clansman. Iwai unleashed a full-auto barrage, but it was too soon. Too short. Too much. The bullets clanged into metal and chipped wood, but they were nowhere near their target.

And their target was dead-on.

Bolan triggered one 3-round burst that cored the clansman's temple.

The rifle dropped from Kobayushi's hand as he lurched uncontrollably toward the warrior. He looked up at Bolan with a strange bewildered gaze, as if he'd known that somehow despite all the precautions they'd taken and ambushes they'd prepared, he'd see the Executioner like this—through the eyes of a dying man.

Kobayushi was gone now, catching up to the clansmen who'd gone before him, their lifeless bodies spread out on the deck.

Mack Bolan felt little remorse for the fallen men. Their time was past. They were soldiers in a secret army, or more exactly, sailors in a secret fleet. They'd come out gunning for him, thinking they'd had him outnumbered. Outnumbered, yeah, Bolan thought, but not outfought.

And now he was the only man moving aboard the ship, piloting the vessel back to the island.

The first part of the attack had worked to the last man. Now it was time for the unconventional stage of the mission, going against the gods themselves.

Rough seas dwarfed the trawler as it neared the shore. It crested a tall wave, then pitched low into a deep trough. The ocean's watery grasp pulled down on the ship, smacking the deck with a heavy splash. When the ship leveled out once more, Bolan guided it toward the same spot where he'd boarded it so long ago.

Kobayushi had taken the fishing trawler out to look for Bolan, unaware that his prey was already aboard. The warrior had slipped onto the trawler while it was anchored in the harbor of the Yamishima fishing village. His approach was totally unnoticed. While the clansmen were always quick to scan the horizon for a distant ship when they were out in the Pacific, they hardly ever glanced at the waters closer to home.

A police patrol boat had dropped Bolan off at sea. His swimming skills did the rest. The long-duration shallow-depth scuba gear gave him the necessary time to make it into the harbor undetected. With a three-hour supply of air, the lightweight Seapak 25 was designed for silent military operations. Working in shallow depths, Bolan only had to wait until the coast was clear.

He'd scaled the side of the trawler, then stowed away in one of the fishing holds. Since the ship was looking for another kind of catch, he was reasonably sure he'd be safe in there. But just in case someone stumbled into the hole, he'd surrounded himself with canvas and netting.

Then he'd waited until the night came, until the storm took hold and the men on board were weary of their assignment. Then the Executioner had emerged from the hold, literally the last thing on their minds.

It was exactly as Haruki had warned him. Iwai Kobayashi had manned the ship with a crew of killers who planned to intercept him on his way in.

The challenge would be ended, and Taro Kuro could renew his attack on less-dangerous prey from JEICO.

But now he'd have to meet Bolan. Daylight was approaching as the trawler grew closer to the shore. The Executioner dropped anchor and put on his lightweight scuba gear again. He clambered down the accommodation ladder and sank into the cold water of the Pacific.

Soon the clan would make an important discovery.

Their enemy had arrived.

12

Razor-sharp swords gleamed in the morning sunlight, their blades buried halfway into the dirt. One by one the champions of the clan emerged from their hillside homes and stared at their earth-sheathed swords. They were alarmed by the cries of their fellow clansmen, alarmed by the theft of their weapons during the night.

Unearthly powers were alive on the island.

The stark evidence stared them in the face as sword upon sword formed a gleaming steel gauntlet that led toward Kuro's home.

To the warriors the swords represented their lives. The blades provided a haven for their souls. Their past, present and future could be read in the shining weapons.

The message was clear—that future was dark. Whoever, whatever, had taken their swords in the night could just as easily have taken their lives.

There was only one explanation possible. The gods themselves had descended upon the mountain. Who else could have crept into their cabins undetected? Who else could have muted their martial senses and taken away their bright and gleaming souls?

The Unseen Powers had shown themselves at last.

Another score of clansmen scaled the hill, looking from one champion to the other, looking at the sage who walked among them, his voice deep, his spirit struck with wonder.

"They make themselves known," Haruki declared. "The Unseen Powers point the way." His walking stick accented his words, pointing toward Kuro's lodge, where the chieftain gazed back at him.

"It's time he proved himself to the gods," the old man continued, his voice holding the clansmen in its spell. "The gods want no other warrior but Taro Kuro."

One of the champions stepped forward and reached for his sword.

The serpentine walking stick flashed through the air, striking the man's hand away. "No," Haruki shouted, "the gods of the mountain have sheathed your swords in its heart. Remove them now, and the clan will bleed to death."

The champion stepped back. The old man's words made sense. He'd been their holy man once, and now his soul was awake again. The other champions stepped back from their swords.

Then Haruki looked at the leader of the clan. "There stands the man whose weapon stayed beside him in the night. Taro Kuro has been selected by the powers we worship."

The sage pressed on, his voice rising as the champions nodded their approval. The submerged criticisms of Kuro were rising to the surface at last.

Thanks to the gods, Haruki thought, and thanks to the powder he'd brewed in their tea. With the narcotic mixture holding them in morphinic grip through the night, the old man had been able to slip in and out of their houses to take their swords and plant them in the earth—and plant illusions in their minds.

Kuro gripped the wooden railing that surrounded the deck of his lodge. "Who did this?" he shouted.

"It is the work of the spirits who fell in battle," Haruki replied. "The men who gave their lives for you. Lives you were so ready to take."

"It's a lie! It's trickery, trickery from a traitor!"

With druidic fury the old man pounded his staff into the earth. "Only spirit warriors could accomplish such a thing," he warned. "Only spirits could steal past the senses of our champions."

Kuro stared back at Haruki. It was futile to deny it. Their faith held that the Unseen Powers were alive on the mountain. They guided the course of the sect. To deny their presence now was to deny his rightful role as chieftain.

A heavy silence fell upon the clansmen as each one of them sensed the gods at work around him.

Then the quiet was shattered by a call from below. An out-of-breath man ran uphill, shouting about the boat in the harbor.

A boat full of ghosts.

The trawler had been found with all its dead passengers aboard. Iwai Kobayushi was captaining a crew of spirits.

"He is here now," the sage shouted. "The Executioner has arrived."

As word of the slaughter spread through the crowd, Kuro called out to his champions, but they refused to listen.

He called out to the other clansmen, and a small group of men headed uphill. They were mostly younger men, fervent loyalists groomed by Kuro for just such a moment as this. None were champions. Fighters, yes. Gunmen and enforcers. But not one of them could stand up to the Executioner.

Yukiko came out of the lodge and stood behind Kuro.

An angry murmur spread through the crowd gathering around the champions. No longer was Yukiko the sacred vessel of the Unseen Powers. As if a spell had been lifted, they saw her as she really was, a malevolent mistress who'd bathe in their blood if it would keep her in power.

"We must fight him with everything we have," Kuro shouted.

Haruki shouted him down. "*You* must fight him. You alone. Not your bandits, not your killers. Taro Kuro himself. That is how the gods will speak to us. If you were right in leading us on this bloody crusade, the Executioner will die. If not, you will fall."

Kuro measured the stony gazes of his champions and the clansmen who stood behind them. Then he looked at his small band of fanatics.

"Accept the challenge you've issued to others," the old man said, "and redeem yourself in the eyes of the gods."

Kuro bowed sharply, accepting the verdict. He had no choice. His eyes fell upon Haruki, promising vengeance when the challenge was over.

Then he looked into the eyes of the Executioner.

The black-clad American walked steadily up the hill, moving quickly past the gauntlet of swords, past the throng of clansmen who stepped back to let him pass.

BOLAN WATCHED the clansmen with his peripheral vision as he waded through their ranks. They stood like ancient statues, only their eyes moving as he threaded his way through the swords posted into the hill. He moved with the bold stride of a man who belonged there, a man placed in their midst by Fate.

Though he had the holstered Beretta and a magazine-laden combat vest, he wasn't fool enough to think he could defeat a clan single-handed.

He had two allies on the island. The sage had done his part already, and Haimyo was doing his part now. Concealed in the woods, the Japanese was in constant radio contact with Mako Tamura's seaborne troops.

Bolan knew what was at stake. If he lost, Kuro would have a stranglehold on the clan, and more blood would flow.

But if Bolan defeated Kuro, he defeated their desire to continue the war against JEICO. Kuro's old guard would fall, and Haruki could steer the sect back on course.

He climbed the stone steps terraced in the hillside, then stood at the bottom of the glass-walled pagoda. A quartet of loyalists barred his way.

"I'm here at your master's invitation," the warrior growled. "Stand aside."

The guards parted.

Bolan proceeded to the landing where Kuro waited for him.

The chieftain wore a traditional black robe, alive with gold-painted dragons. His hair was freshly cut, a dagger-sharp peak running down his forehead. He folded his arms in front of him and waited.

"You know why I'm here," Bolan said.

Kuro studied him with a regal gaze. "You give honor to your lord, whoever it is. Certainly not the hollow men of your government. Nor could a warrior on his own get this far. Before we begin, tell me who shaped you. Who trained you in this way?"

"My Aunt Tilly," Bolan replied. "Let's just do it, guy."

Anger flared on the man's face, just as Bolan had calculated. Rather than accept the warrior myths Kuro wove around himself, Bolan was ready for war.

"You came bearing arms," Kuro pointed out.

"It's a foolish man who walks into the camp of his enemy without a weapon. Especially when that man has shown his false colors so many times before."

The veil lifted from Kuro's eyes. No longer did charm lurk there. Hate burned hotly as he stepped aside and gestured toward the main entrance.

Bolan passed through, eyes alert, scanning the room. The floor shone like gold, the wooden slats polished smooth. Around the wall hung ancient implements of the warrior's art. Staff, scythe, halberd and *chigiriki,* a spiked ball and chain attached to a long staff. They were simple weapons with complex maneuvers. At least in that respect Kuro followed the old traditions.

Kuro stepped into his sanctum and closed the door behind him. He spoke softly, almost hypnotically, but Bolan paid little attention to words. Instead, he gauged the other man's eyes, reading his mind through the glinting hate. Though he was talking calmly, there was a chance he'd erupt into violence at any moment.

"Enough talk," Bolan said, cutting off Kuro's attempt to distract him. "It's a simple bargain. If you die, the clan stops harassing the JEICO."

"And if you die, then the company will have to open its coffers to us. Yes, very simple. I'll look forward to collecting."

Bolan unholstered the Beretta, unsnapped his combat vest and set them on the floor.

Kuro removed his robe, revealing a scarred torso that told of a hundred cuts. His chest was chiseled muscle, and his stomach was flat. The edge of his palms and his knuckles were callused. He hadn't sat idle while the clan fought his battles. He was in excellent fighting shape.

The clansman glided across the room toward the weapon racks, Bolan close behind.

In tandem the warriors reached for the hardwood bos, twirling the long staffs overhead like mirror images as they faced each other.

Kuro whirled to his right, changed his grip and then swung the staff at the Executioner's feet.

Bolan jumped to avoid the sweep, and then came the real attack. At the end of his swing, Kuro turned away from the warrior, cocked his hands and slid the bo beneath his elbow. The blunt end shot straight for his adversary's head.

The Executioner levered the bo in an upward arc that pushed aside the stick. Then, sliding it down along Kuro's deflected weapon, Bolan brought the staff down on his face like an ax. The strike angered Kuro more than it hurt him, though the side of his face wore the red imprint of the staff.

He retaliated with a lightning-fast broadside to Bolan's left hip. Then, a split second later he whipped the other end of the bo toward the warrior's neck. Bolan deflected it at the last moment, but the staff cracked him hard on the jaw.

Kuro was quicker with the bo, but Bolan had a longer reach with his legs. Instead of launching another attack with the staff, the Executioner turned to his right and powered a side thrust kick with his left foot.

It caught Kuro square in the knee, locking his right leg for a painful second. Temporarily immobilized by the blow, Kuro lost his center. Bolan followed through with a right snap kick.

Kuro's left hand swept low, circling around Bolan's ankle and flinging his foot to the floor with a loud thud. As the warrior's inertia turned his body, the clan leader gripped the staff again and poleaxed him in the middle of the back.

Bolan went rigid as the pain shot through him. He had only a few seconds left before the shock traveled all the way through his body and left him open to a final attack.

Willing his hands to hold on to the staff, the Executioner spun and charged Kuro with both hands in front of him. He clotheslined him in the neck, pushed up, then forced him backward with the staff at his throat.

Kuro screamed, the sharp yell expelling his air before he was pinned to the wall.

A knee smashed into Bolan's rib cage, then a sharp-toed kick gouged into his shin.

But the Executioner held on while rainbows of pain lit up his screaming nerve ends. He pushed up with all of his strength, pressing Kuro off his feet and back against the wall.

The clansman's bo bounced to the floor as he released the weapon and freed his hands.

A rock-hard fist powered upward and slammed into the underside of Bolan's jaw, and he tasted the salty copper taste of blood as it sprayed from his mouth. Kuro's eyes flashed with hope at the sight of blood, as if it were a fountain of youth that gave him back his strength.

Bolan pushed harder against Kuro's neck and throttled him with the bo.

A spear hand chopped into Bolan's side, just missing his heart. Though he had Kuro pinned, the man was still capable of killing him.

Bolan reared his head back, took another uppercut to his numbed and bloody jaw, then snapped forward suddenly, ramming his head into Kuro's breastbone. There was a cracking sound, and the chieftain turned sideways, the shattered bones inside his body guiding his motions.

The Executioner stepped back and released the bo, letting Kuro's feet touch the ground again. On the way down, his hand gouged for Bolan's eyes but stopped suddenly.

That was the instant that the Executioner's hammerfists pounded on top of the man's head as if he were driving home a railroad spike. The blow crushed the clansman's skull and freed his soul.

Kuro was dead by the time he reached the floor.

Bolan stepped outside the lodge and onto the deck to the shocked and strangled cries of the crowd.

A jagged column of clansmen drifted away from the hilltop, most of them loyalists to Kuro.

The champions of the sect stood their ground, staring at the Executioner. A few of them fell in behind Haruki as he climbed up the stone steps to take the place of Taro Kuro.

The silver-haired sage stood atop the stairs to face the clansmen and spoke in a soft but powerful voice whose cadence was now the beating heart of the Unseen Powers.

As the loyalists dropped from sight, Bolan went back into the house and gathered his gear.

YUKIKO SPRINTED DOWNHILL, leaping over the rocks and gullies that bordered the treeline. The light-footed goddess cradled an automatic weapon that looked outsize in her arms, almost as if she were a child playing with a toy gun.

But it wasn't a toy, and she knew how to use it.

She stopped at a spear point of forest with a commanding view of the slope, swung the barrel of the automatic carbine to the left and planted her feet on the ground.

Then she burned off a 30-round clip of 5.56 mm ammo. The chatter of the CAR-15 echoed in the hills—and so did the sudden cries of the wounded. A handful of clansmen dropped to the ground, one of them for good. She'd fired from left to right, the uphill barrage digging up spouts of earth at their feet and fountains of blood from their bodies.

The man who'd been fatally hit had tumbled backward, legs rising in the air as if he'd been yanked off his feet by the Unseen Powers. He'd faced everything the clan had sent him against over the years—only to die at the hands of Kuro's mistress.

No longer was she their goddess.

Now she was fair game.

The remaining champions had seen the carbine flash, and suddenly they were no longer easy targets. To a man they picked up their weapons and headed for cover.

Yukiko slapped another 30-round clip into the rifle and retreated into the dense woods.

The champions were coming.

CURRENTS OF WIND FLOWED through the tall grass, kicking up peaks and troughs of green waves as the Sea King choppers descended onto the hilltop.

Mako Tamura stood in the doorway of the first aircraft giving the go-ahead to the unit of flak-jacketed commandos leaping to the ground.

He'd brought in three choppers from the destroyer cruising off the eastern coast of Hokkaido. The assault team was made up of handpicked Security Bureau men and seasoned troops from the Japanese Maritime Self-Defense Force.

Dust and debris scattered in the downwash from the rotors as the troops hit the ground.

A cluster of Kuro loyalists opened up with automatic weapons until the door gunner ripped them with a hundred rounds from the M-60. While the heavy fire scattered the resistance, teams of disembarked troops set up a rolling barrage of automatic fire as they leap-frogged after the fleeing clansmen.

Tamura directed the mopping-up operation, then saw the Executioner approaching through the cordite mist.

YUKIKO STOPPED RUNNING when she hit a stretch of forest where sharp branches clutched and ripped at her skin and the trees grew at chaotic angles. Nearly impassable, the terrain forced her to a slow walk.

And then she knew she wasn't alone.

The sounds of leaves rustling on the forest floor grew rapid, as if a small animal were burrowing nearby.

For one brief moment she saw the clansman as he sprang from cover and hurtled past a gap in the trees. He was short and powerfully built, looking like one of the Ainu warriors who'd originally inhabited this part of Japan. He seemed a primitive spirit at home in the wilds, at home with the long curved bow he wielded.

Yukiko dropped back and angled for a better position. She triggered a short burst from the CAR-15 that shredded the bark from the tree the bowman had ducked behind.

But she knew she'd missed him. She fired too late and too wild.

As the woman stalked through the spindly woods toward her adversary's hiding place, she heard another clansman coming up behind her. She looked over her shoulder and caught a flash of steel and a glimpse of glistening feral eyes.

Then the second man vanished.

Yukiko knew it ended here. She wouldn't leave the island like the others. The loyalists who supported Kuro to the end had planned ahead of time to cut down the opposing clansmen. Failing that, they'd gather near the harbor and escape from the island.

Money waited for them in secret accounts in Tokyo, Singapore and Hong Kong. Kuro had planned well in the event he was deposed. If the rebelling clansmen were victorious, the loyalists planned on taking their faith and their fortune with them.

But now the survivors would be minus one goddess.

She could hear the sounds of the pursuit growing closer, rapid footsteps that spiked her heartbeat, slashing branches whipping back into place as the woodsmen closed in on her. And then their voices called out to her to stand and fight.

She had drawn blood, and now she would have to repay it.

The warriors were taking back control of the clan by taking her life.

Yukiko screamed, then stepped forward, turned left and fired a burst.

The stream of lead cut through the woods, chopping branches and brush. But not flesh and bone.

Then she heard a whistling sound. A razor-sharp arrow sliced through her throat and jerked her off her feet, the thin wooden arrow shaft sprouting from her neck as it slammed her back against a tree.

The steel arrowhead had ripped through the back of her throat and pinned her to the tree as her life slipped rapidly away.

The second clansman appeared in front of her, wielding a sword. She saw the glint of sun on **steel** as it swung in a wicked arc toward her neck.

And then she saw nothing at all.

THE SEA KING CHOPPER droned behind the powerboat like an angry wasp, darting left and right to evade the stream of automatic fire from the forty footer.

Two clansmen fired wildly from the bridge, constantly thrown off balance by the bucking movements of the craft as it zigzagged away from the helicopter.

A clansman propped himself between the cabin and the railing on the side deck, firing controlled bursts at the Sea King, his on-target volleys clinking and clanging against the chopper's armored shell.

As the helicopter snaked above the churning wake of the powerboat, Mako Tamura flicked on the transmitter connected to a bank of loudspeakers on the aircraft's underside. His voice boomed as he gave the pilot of the boat one last chance to stop.

But the vessel continued on, their answer coming in the sustained burst of gunfire aimed at the chopper.

Tamura nodded at Bolan, who sat in the door gunner's seat, wearing flak vest and helmet and holding on to the belt-fed M-60. Three other commandos the security chief had rapidly selected to join in the pursuit of the fleeing clansmen edged toward the doorway with grenade launchers in hand.

The chopper surged forward as the pilot made his pass.

Bolan let loose with the M-60, pouring heavy-metal rain onto the boat. As the 7.62 mm loads strafed the deck, several clansmen fell back with a fatal strip of lead stitching them from hip to head.

A trio of gunners still tracked the metal bird—until an incendiary grenade thumped into the fuel tank. A tidal wave of flame roiled over the ship as it blew, metal fragments spearing the sky while the Sea King banked to the right.

It made one more pass and hovered over the maelstrom of wreckage, but nothing had survived the explosion. The last of the rogue clansmen were gone, phantoms followed in Taro Kuro's wake.

The chopper rose and headed out to sea where Hal Brognola waited for them aboard a U.S. Navy cutter. Tamura raised him on the radio, then handed the mike to Bolan.

The Executioner looked back at the island that was now firmly under control. Like an unseen power himself, he'd played his hand. It was time to go.

Go for a hair-raising ride in

JAMES AXLER

DEATH LANDS

Dark Carnival

Trapped in an evil baron's playground, the rides are downhill and dangerous for Ryan Cawdor and his roving band of warrior-survivalists.

For one brief moment after their narrow escape, Ryan thinks they have found the peace and idyll they so desperately seek. But a dying messenger delivers a dark message....

When terrorism stalks the free world,
retribution is swift—and hard.

DON PENDLETON's

STONY MAN IV

Stony Man Farm—a sophisticated command base hidden deep
in the Virginia forest where America's elite combat specialists are
forged into a hard-hitting, tactical defense unit. Mack Bolan, Able
Team and Phoenix Force work within and beyond the law, ready
to deliver justice anywhere at the command of the President.

As America is propelled toward a deadly showdown in the shifting sands of the Middle East, Stony Man is put on red alert.

Bolan goes to the front lines of a weapons war.

DON PENDLETON's

MACK BOLAN®

FIREPOWER

The American defense industry has been dealt a deadly blow. Dirty men with dirty money are out for the kind of control that breaches national security.

Bolan finds himself in the middle of a war with no clear line of fire. For the Executioner, it's time to take out the enemy—shot by shot.

The Guardian Strikes

David North

A cloud of deadly gas is about to settle, and then a madman's dreams for a perfect society will be fulfilled. Behind it all is a sinister being searching for life-giving energy. He is the last of an ancient godlike race called the Guardians, and his survival hinges on the annihilation of the Earth's population.

Standing between him and survival are two men—the former CIA counterinsurgency specialist and the swordsman from the mists of time. Once again they join forces across time to defeat the savage being determined to destroy both their worlds.

Look for THE GUARDIAN STRIKES, Book 3 of the Gold Eagle miniseries TIME WARRIORS.